MW00623400

Perfect Harmony

by Andrew Grosso
and The Essentials

SAMUEL
FRENCH

FOUNDED 1830

SAMUELFRENCH.COM
SAMUELFRENCH-LONDON.CO.UK

FOR PRODUCTION ENQUIRIES

UNITED STATES AND CANADA
Info@SamuelFrench.com
1-866-598-8449

UNITED KINGDOM AND EUROPE
Plays@SamuelFrench-London.co.uk
020-7255-4302

Each title is subject to availability from Samuel French, depending upon country of performance. Please be aware that *PERFECT HARMONY* may not be licensed by Samuel French in your territory. Professional and amateur producers should contact the nearest Samuel French office or licensing partner to verify availability.

MUSIC USE NOTE

The performance rights for music contained within the licensee's rented score are granted by the license agreement between Samuel French and the licensee. For music used during pre-show, intermission between Acts, or otherwise, licensees are solely responsible for obtaining formal written permission from copyright owners to use copyrighted music during the performance of this play and are strongly cautioned to do so. If no such permission is obtained by the licensee, then the licensee must use only original music that the licensee owns and controls. Licensees are solely responsible and liable for all music clearances and shall indemnify the copyright owners of the play and their licensing agent, Samuel French, against any costs, expenses, losses and liabilities arising from the use of music by licensees. Please contact the appropriate music licensing authority in your territory for the rights to any incidental music.

IMPORTANT BILLING AND CREDIT
REQUIREMENTS

All producers of *PERFECT HARMONY* must give credit to the author of the play in all programs distributed in connection with performances of the play, and in all instances in which the title of the play appears for the purposes of advertising, publicizing or otherwise exploiting the play and/ or a production. The name of the author must appear on a separate line on which no other name appears, immediately following the title and must appear in size of type not less than fifty percent of the size of the title type. In all programs distributed in connection with performances of the play, the name of the original Off Broadway producers must appear on a separate line and must appear in size and type not less than twenty-five percent of the size of the title type. Billing must be substantially as follows:

(NAME OF PRODUCER)

presents

PERFECT HARMONY (100%)
By Andrew Grosso & The Essentials (50%)

Originally Produced Off Broadway in New York City
by Michael Musto, Elissa Burke, Alec Stais and Joshua P. Weiss (25%)

Licensees shall be required to give the following credit (in size and prominence of type no less than that used for the designers' credit) on the main credit page of all theatre programs when Adam Wachter's vocal arrangements are utilized:

Arrangements by Adam Wachter

Licensees shall be required to give the following credit (in size and prominence of type no less than that used for the designers' credit) on the main credit page of all theatre programs when vocal arrangements by Ray Bailey and Jeremy Gussin are utilized:

Additional Arrangements by Ray Bailey and Jeremy Gussin

IMPORTANT BILLING AND CREDIT
REQUIREMENTS

"I Think We're Alone Now"
By Richard Rosenblatt
Used by permission of EMI Longitude Music
Arranged by Adam Wachter

"I Want You Back"
By Freddie Perren, Alphonso J. Mizell, Berry Gordy, Jr.
Used by permission of Jobete Music Co. Inc.
Arranged by Adam Wachter

"Mony Mony"
By Bobby Bloom, Tommy James, Richard Rosenblatt, Bo Gentry
Used by permission of EMI Longitude Music
Arranged by Adam Wachter

"My Life Flows On in Endless Song / How Can I Keep from Singing?"
By Robert Wadsworth Lowry
Arranged by Adam Wachter

"Sexual Healing"
By Marvin P. Gaye, David Ritz, Odell Elliot Brown
Used by permission of EMI April Music Inc., EMI Blackwood Music Inc.
Arranged by Adam Wachter

"Three Times A Lady"
By Lionel Richie
Used by Permission of Jobete Music Co. Inc.
Arranged by Jeremy Gussin

"We Belong"
By David Eric Lowen, Daniel Anthony Navarro
Used by permission of Screen Gems-EMI Music Inc.
Arranged by Adam Wachter

"What I Like About You"
By Walter Palamarchuk, Jimmy Marinos, Mike Skill
Used by permission of EMI April Music Inc.
Arranged by Adam Wachter

Please note that when "Hooked On A Feeling" is used, the following musical composition credit must replace the musical composition credit for "Sexual Healing":

"Hooked On A Feeling"
By Mark James
Used by Permission of Screen Gems-EMI Music Inc.
Arranged by Jeremy Gussin

IMPORTANT BILLING AND CREDIT REQUIREMENTS

PERFECT HARMONY was created at NYU Graduate Acting's Studio Tisch program, premiered at FringeNYC in 2006, had an extended run at the Fringe Encore Series, reopened Off-Off Broadway at the Clurman Theatre in 2008, and had a successful Off Broadway run at Theatre Row's Acorn Theatre in 2010 after a preview period at 45 Bleecker Theatre and a run at the Stoneham Theatre, in Stoneham, Massachusetts.

The Off Broadway production of *PERFECT HARMONY* (Michael Musto, Elissa Burke, Alec Stais and Joshua P. Weiss, Producers) was directed by Andrew Grosso with vocal arrangements and musical direction by Ray Bailey and Adam Wachter, sets by Nick Francone, costumes by Becky Lasky, and lighting by Brian Jones. Casting was by Geoff Josselson. Props were provided by Emily Nichols. Lisa Loen was the assistant costume designer, and Seth Reiser was the associate lighting designer. The press representative was Jim Baldassare, with advertising and marketing by The Pekoe Group. The Production Stage Manager was William E. Cruttenden III and Erin Maureen Koster, with Nathan K. Claus as the assistant stage manager. The cast was as follows:

MELODY MCDANIELS.	Dana Acheson
VALERIE SMOOTER	Faryl Amadeus
JASPER MERGH / DR. LARRY MERGH	Clayton Apgar
KERRI TAYLOR / TOBI MCCLINTOCH.	Marie-France Arcilla
SIMON DEPARDIEU / GORAN DHIARDEUBOVIC	David Barlow
MICHAELA "MICKEY D" DHIARDEUBOVIC / . . .	Kate Morgan Chadwick
KIKI TUNE	
JB SMOOTER / JESUS	Jarid Faubel
PHILIP FELLOWES V.	Kobi Libii
MEGHAN BEANS	Kelly McCreary
LASSITER A. JAYSON III	Robbie Collier Sublett

Tate Evans understudied each of the Ladies in Red and Marshall York understudied each of the Acafellas.

Thank you to Prasanth Akkapeddi, Anne & Mahlon Apgar IV, Inbal Arie, Jason Aschenbrand, Andrew Bauer, Frank Blake, Mary & John Brock III, Richard DelBello, H. Allen Hall Jr., Macy & Robert Lasky, Dean Mann, Devin Mann, Sheri Telanoff, Meredith & Henry Von Kohorn, and Helen & Ken Weiss.

PRODUCTION HISTORY

The original 2005 cast for the first production at Studio Tisch at NYU included:

MELODY MCDANIELS . . . . .Autumn Dornfeld

JASPER MERGH / DR. LARRY MERGH . . . . Blake Whyte

SIMON DEPARDIEU / GORAN DHIARDEUBOVIC . . . . .David Barlow

PHILIP FELLOWES V . . . . Santino Fontana

JB SMOOTER / JERRY WEINER/ JESUS . . . . .Scott Janes

LASSITER A. JAYSON III / GERALD STUDMAN . . . . .Jeff Binder

MEGHAN BEANS . . . . Maria Ramirez

VALERIE SMOOTER . . . . Margie Stokley

KERRI TAYLOR / TOBI MCCLINTOCH . . . . Marina Squerciatti

MICHAELA "MICKEY D" DHIARDEUBOVIC / . . . . .Jeanine Serralles
KIKI TUNE

The 2008 cast for the Clurman Theatre production included:

MELODY MCDANIELS . . . . .Dana Acheson

JASPER MERGH / DR. LARRY MERGH. . . . . .Clayton Apgar

SIMON DEPARDIEU / GORAN DHIARDEUBOVIC . . . . .Sean Dugan

PHILIP FELLOWES V . . . . .Benjamin Huber

JB SMOOTER / JESUS . . . . .Scott Janes

LASSITER A. JAYSON III . . . . Vayu O'Donnell

MEGHAN BEANS . . . . .Amy Rutberg

VALERIE SMOOTER. . . . . Margie Stokley

KERRI TAYLOR / TOBI MCCLINTOCH . . . . Nisi Sturgis

MICHAELA "MICKEY D" DHIARDEUBOVIC / KIKI TUNE. . . . Kathy Searle

UNDERSTUDY FOR THE LADIES IN RED . . . . Tate Evans

TIME & PLACE

A few years ago, at a prep school a few towns away. Maybe New England.

CAST OF CHARACTERS

The Acafellas (and auditioning students)

LASSITER A. JAYSON III . . . . Senior. He is the Pitch and an artist
PHILIP FELLOWES V . . . . Senior
JASPER MERGH . . . . Junior
JB SMOOTER . . . . Senior
SIMON DEPARDIEU . . . . Freshman, auditioning for the group

Ladies in Red / Lady Treble

MELODY MCDANIELS . . . . Senior. She is the Pitch and President
MICHAELA "MICKEY D" DHIARDEAUBOVIC . . . . Sophomore
VALERIE SMOOTER . . . . Sophomore
MEGHAN BEANS . . . . Junior
KERRI TAYLOR . . . . Sophomore. The Team Manager

Members of The Greater Community
(with Suggested Doubling from Ensemble)

DR. LARRY MERGH . . . . The School Psychologist (**JASPER**)
KIKI TUNE . . . . Talent Manager (**MICKEY D**)
GORAN DHIARDEAUBOVIC . . . Older brother of, and legal guardian to,
Michaela (**SIMON**)
TOBY MCCLINTOCH . . . . Vocal Therapist (**KERRI**)
ANNOUNCER . . . . MC, National High School A Cappella
Championships (**JB**)
OTHERS . . . . Stage Managers & Run Crew at Nationals (**VARIOUS**)

NOTES ON STAGING

While most of the play takes place in spaces like the Music Room and Fellowes Auditorium, there are additional moments at downstage microphones wherein the characters directly address the audience and speak as if offering public testimony at a school-community assembly.

The projections indicated in bold can be cast onto any surface appropriate for your set (such as a chalkboard in the Music Room) and should be legible to the audience.

When a character's line of dialogue is interrupted by another character's line after an en-dash (–), it indicates a momentary interruption of, and pause in, the first speaker's line.

The play should be staged fluidly, cutting seamlessly from one speaker or scene to the next without any pauses in action.

The play was written to be performed in one act, but if you need an intermission, one can be inserted immediately prior to Kiki Tune's initial entrance.

If you wish to perform this play for younger or more sensitive audiences, language changes have been included in the Appendix at the back of the script. The Appendix also includes modified scenes for **KIKI TUNE** and **GORAN**, as well as a replacement song in lieu of "Sexual Healing".

Scene One

(A projection reads, **"The Alma Mater. Music by Lassiter A. Jayson I. Words by Philip Fellowes IV"**. *From the darkened stage, we hear the sound of a pitchpipe blowing a single note, then* **MELODY** *giving the pitches, followed by a whispered "With pride" and a quick "one two three and". Then we hear* **THE ACAFELLAS** *and the* **LADIES IN RED** *sing the first stanza to "The Alma Mater". It was written by* **LASSITER** *and* **PHILIP** *'s grandfathers. It was a time before the school went co-ed; it's unclear as to whether the lyrics have ever been officially updated to reflect that.)*

[MUSIC NO. 1: THE ALMA MATER]

(Lights still up on **DR**. **MERGH***. The projection reads,* **"Dr. Larry Mergh, School Psychologist"***.)*

DR. **MERGH**. You can't keep them from singing. And why would you want to? They've won 18 national championships, they inspired that TV show, they've sung at the White House, and they sound perfect. The Acafellas of course. Though the girls try very hard as well. But as their guidance counselor, as a parent, and as someone who's sung under the harsh lights at Nationals myself, it's my job not to ignore the con side of this perfection. The pressure. In basketball, they don't raise the rims every year. But with a cappella, the vise grip tightens with every concert. God, with this tight harmony singing, if you're one of the boys in the group, or one of the Ladies in Red too, of course, though they've never won, if you sing one wrong note, or miss a pitch by a fraction of a half-step, or breathe just a eighth note too soon, the entire group is thrown off. You don't just undermine your own performance.

No. You've ruined everyone in the group's performance! It's your fault! You did it! A cappella is a cult of pressure and perfection. It's a hungry beast and now, this year with these developments, it's claiming its victims!

Scene Two

(**THE ACAFELLAS** *perform "Get Ready" by The Temptations, for an auditorium full of auditioning freshmen. The song was a hit when it came out, a hit again in the nineties, and the boys in* **THE ACAFELLAS** *are quite certain they are making it a hit again every time they sing it. Regardless, they do sound pretty great.*)

[MUSIC NO. 2: "GET READY"]

(*Song finishes and* **THE ACAFELLAS** *immediately address the audience directly as if they were auditioning freshman. The projection reads,* "**Acaditions**".)

LASSITER. Hi, I'm Lassiter A. Jayson the Third.

PHILIP. I'm Philip Fellowes the Fifth.

JB. Hey, I'm JB.

ALL. And we're the Acafellas!

PHILIP. Fellows.

JB & LASSITER. Fellas.

JB. Hey, this is Jasper. He may not talk, but he's got the best voice in the group.

(**JASPER** *humbly shakes his head "no".*)

LASSITER. Maybe after Philip.

PHILIP. JB, tell Lassiter thanks, but it's his arrangements that make me sound amazing.

JB. Maybe just once, he could arrange a bass solo. (*The other* **ACAFELLAS** *laugh.*) That dude at Country Day sang one.

PHILIP. Focus. And they came in second.

LASSITER. Actually, (*to audience*) this year, we will be doing an entirely new repertoire. (*to* **THE ACAFELLAS**) I'm throwing out all the old songs.

JB. What?

PHILIP. Lassiter's arrangements new and old, both of which we'll be singing this year, are works of art; they win.

JB. Dude, I hear the judges really wanna hear a spoken word slow jam – *(He has proposed this before.)*

LASSITER.	**PHILIP**.
(simultaneously cutting off JB)	*(simultaneously cutting off JB)*
We are not doing a slow jam spoken word interlude.	We are never speaking.

LASSITER. Next.

*(Lights up on **SIMON** in the audience, waiting to audition. He address the audience directly.)*

SIMON. Hi. I'm Simon DePardieu and I'm super-duper not nervous about my acadition. And if I *was* anxious, I know that's just my bodies way of oh no – saying – no, I'm relax – ow, not now, please ooww!

*(**SIMON** fights through pain spasms to use his inhaler. Lights back up on **THE ACAFELLAS**.)*

PHILIP. Lassiter's the pitchpipe –

JB. – the dude who conducts and writes all the songs.

LASSITER. Arranges. And only some of them.

PHILIP. Lassiter's father –

JB. *(to **LASSITER**)* Arranged! Dude, you basically wrote the Bon Jovi Medley.

PHILIP. – was the pitch as well, and Lassiter's grandfather, who was one of the original Acafounders, was the first pitchpipe. And now Lassiter has been pitch too. And when we have – he has a son, maybe he will have been pitch too as well someday.

LASSITER. Frankly, it's time we stopped singing so many cheesy '80s pop songs.

PHILIP.	**JB**.
But the judges love those.	Old people love '80s music.

*(**JASPER** nods.)*

PHILIP. The Acafellas have always had a tradition of doing the popular songs of the day. That's one of the things that's helped us win Nationals. Generation after generation.

LASSITER. *(to audience)* It's not about winning.

PHILIP. *(to audience)* But it's not not about winning.

LASSITER. JB, can you tell Philip, I know it's not about not winning. But –

PHILIP. JB, can you tell Lassiter I know it's not just about winning. But winning –

LASSITER. Is not what it's about, thank you. You know, if we spend all our time singing what the audience wants to hear, then we're not spending any time singing what they need to hear. Okay? Thank you. Next.

JB. I know what you're thinking; those guys are like Olympic level music dorks, what if they think I suck? But, before I joined, the only singing I'd ever done was at Chloe Chapin's karaoke sweet sixteen before she got knocked –

PHILIP. JB, focus.

JB. – and they've been super patient. So, relax.

LASSITER. Next.

(Lights change to **SIMON**.*)*

SIMON. Oh God, I haven't slept for like four days. My eyes are so stingy. I've wanted to be an Acafella for so long. My acadition song is a little unusual but my mom says that'll just help me stand out and be remembered. She says I have a great voice.

(Lights back on **THE ACAFELLAS**.*)*

LASSITER. It's not just whether you have a great voice.

SIMON: Oh no. *(He puffs on his inhaler.)*

LASSITER. There are considerations. Can you read music? One. Can you hold your own part? Two. Three – and this should probably be one – can you blend? If you can't blend your voice into the sound of the guys singing next to you, it stands out like a sixth finger.

PHILIP. Or toe. I remember when I was a freshman sitting in your seats, getting into this group meant the world to me. My grandfather, Philip Fellows the Fourth – *(beat)* OK, I'm Phillip Fellows the Fifth, my father, Phillip Fellows the Fourth, and my grandfather, the first Phillip Fellows the Fourth, had a falling out over an issue. And my father, Philip Fellows the Fourth, reclaimed – see he was originally also Phillip Fellows the Fifth – but he reclaimed Phillip Fellows the Fourth and I have now become Philip Fellows the For – Fifth – Okay, my grandfather, Phillip Fellows the Fourth the First, along with Lassiter's grandfather, created and founded the Acafellows.

JB. *(corrects him)* Acaditions are really just a chance to get to know the guys and shit –

PHILIP. Focus. That's the language that almost cost us Regionals.

JB. *(to PHILIP)* But it didn't. *(to audience)* Make sure you'll fit in and shit.

LASSITER. Okay. Next.

(Lights back on SIMON.)

SIMON. I have these really bad canker sores. There are so many. Stress provokes them. I take *(shows his inhaler)* FlemCort to numb the pain, only it's a topical steroid, so sometimes it stimulates my jaw muscles too much, and I get lockjaw, which feels like a steel trap on a little beaver's leg. This stops the grinding. *(inserts mouthguard)*

(Lights back up on PHILIP addressing the audience.)

PHILIP. Lassiter and I, uh, don't really speak. The reason my grandfather and father had the falling out had to do with Lassiter's grandfather. And my grandfather. They were, uh, very close. And when that got discovered, my father disowned my grandfather and so out of respect for my father and for his anger and because he made me swear a solemn oath not to, I don't speak to Lassiter. We're still totally best friends. And most of the times one of the guys is around to translate, and when we sing together, we can just look across the room and know we understand each other.

LASSITER. Next.

(Lights shift to **THE ACAFELLAS** *inside the Music Room. Enter* **SIMON**.*)*

LASSITER. Hey, welcome, uh, *(looks at list of names)* Simon. *(pronounces it "Sigh Mun")*

SIMON. Simon. *(as in "Sih Moan")*

PHILIP. On the signup sheet, it's Simon. *(as in "Sigh Mun")*

SIMON. It's French.

JB. It's gonna make high school rough. Hey, I'm JB.

SIMON. You're my favorite, after Jasper. *(to* **JASPER***)* Are you really mute?

LASSITER, PHILIP, JB. He's not mute –

LASSITER. – he just thinks words are insufficient.

PHILIP. – he's just not allowed to talk.

JB. He's just quiet, and shit.

*(***SIMON** *looks at* **JASPER**. **JASPER** *nods at* **SIMON**.*)*

PHILIP. Uh, guys, focus, we've got a schedule.

SIMON. The title of my song is entitled for my mother –

JB: Oh dude.

SIMON. – I'm a little nervous. I didn't realize the room was going to be so big. *(referencing the audience)*

LASSITER. What note can I give you?

SIMON. I brought my own.

(He pulls out a harmonica and blows himself a B, but the vibrations cause a spasm of mouth pain.)

OWWW *(sings a "B" again)* B *(another spasm of pain)* OWWWW.

LASSITER. Do you want to take a moment?

SIMON. I can do this.

PHILIP. He can go to the Nurse and come back at the end.

SIMON. I can do this… I can do it.

(He sings the Commodore's ballad, "Three Times A Lady" which, although it was a Billboard #1 Hit, a Soul #1 Hit, and even a Country Hit [for Conway Twitty], is still a bit too slow and sappy for **THE ACAFELLAS'** *tastes, particularly* **PHILIP**. **SIMON** *compounds his folly by starting too quietly.)*

SIMON.

THANKS FOR THE TIMES THAT YOU'VE GIVEN ME,

PHILIP. *(spoken)* We can't hear you.

*(***SIMON** *puffs inhaler, his singing is growing louder with each line.)*

[MUSIC NO. 3: "THREE TIMES A LADY"]

(The mouth pain begins to attack him. He fights it off and sings louder and stronger. Like Levi Stubbs singing to Bernadette.)

(The pain spasms bring **SIMON** *to his knees, but he's undaunted, his voice lifted to heaven. It's as if James Brown were suddenly a freshman.)*

*(***THE ACAFELLAS** *are stunned.)*

JB. Dude.

SIMON. *(exiting in terror)* Thank you for the opportunity.

Scene Three

(Lights up on the **LADIES IN RED** *rehearsing in the Music Room. The projection reads,* **"Ladies in Red"***.)*

MELODY. Alright Ladies, One more time from the top. *(blows pitch)* Ladies, with pride.

(They sing the traditional American folks hymn, "My Life Flows On In Endless Song / How Can I Keep From Singing". **MELODY** *leads them flawlessly, if a bit technically and soullessly.* **MEGHAN** *has a hard time containing her exuberance.* **VALERIE** *sings perfectly and happily, except when* **MICKEY***, who sings very few of the correct words, stares at her so that they can come in simultaneously.* **KERRI** *sings along from the sidelines.)*

[MUSIC NO. 4: "MY LIFE FLOWS ON IN ENDLESS SONG / HOW CAN I KEEP FROM SINGING (PRE-PRISE)"]

*(***MELODY** *stops this with…)*

MELODY. *(spoken)* Ladies! Ladies! Ladies!

*(***KERRI** *applauds and hands the girls face towels and water bottles. Enter* **JASPER** *carrying roses.)*

VALERIE.	**MICKEY.**	**MEGHAN.**
Hey. Hey Jasper.	Hello Jasper.	Hi Jasper.

*(***JASPER** *hands flowers to* **MELODY***.)*

MELODY. They've wilted, but we can still use them. Thank you, Jasper. *(pats him)* Thanks. Ladies, we've got work.

KERRI, MICKEY, VALERIE.	**MEGHAN.**
Bye Jasper.	Goodbye Jasper.

MICKEY. *(to* **VALERIE***)* I know your brother, JB, is big meat on campus, but I think Malady's boyfriend is so healthy.

MEGHAN. Hot. So hot. Melody's boyfriend.

MELODY. Ladies!

(During this section, the lights dim on the **LADIES IN RED** *and* **KERRI** *cautiously approaches a microphone. She talks directly to the audience.)*

KERRI. *(spoken)* The Manager's job is to be there; to assist the pitch and be…indispensable; Xeroxing music, getting water, giving fistchomp shoulder rubs, vacuuming out the buttcrack van because dust particles can really scratch the throat. I became manager because… God, I love singing. Eat your face off.

(Pause. She realizes that her tic has acted up. **KERRI** *is not always aware of what words are coming out of her mouth – sometimes they emerges in a conversational voice that matches her normal speech and sometimes they emerge in a much, much darker tone.)*

It's not Tourette's, that's a really inaccurate stereotype. Sometimes words… well, this is how my dad describes it: it's like there's a river, and it's beautiful river, and most kids brains just want to get straight to the other side. But mine just likes to take a look around and pump you in the skull does that make sense?

(Lights shift back to the Music Room scene.)

MELODY. *(Addressing the girls.* **KERRI** *hands* **MELODY** *her note cards and then takes the minutes.)* Okay, Ladies, listening line. Thank you, Kelly –

KERRI*:* Kerri. It's Kerri. Taylor.

*(***MELODY** *ignores* **KERRI***'s correction and powers onward. During her speech she consults her notes on her color coded, highlighted index cards, as she gives her beginning of the year pep talk. Although she is interrupted regularly,* **MELODY** *never loses steam.)*

MELODY. Forget everything you know about the Ladies in Red – This year we are now called –

*(***MELODY** *snaps and the projection changes to read,* "**Lady Treble**"*.)*

– Lady Treble!

(The girls all notice, though not as much a **MELODY** *had hoped they might.)*

MICKEY. We changed name again?

MELODY. Lady Treble, I have a few notes and a major announcement.

VALERIE. Don't look at me. Thanks.

MEGHAN. Oh, I have a suggestion –

MELODY. There will be time for your suggestiveness at the end. Lady Treble –

MEGHAN. Okay, if we're changing the name again, we can also change the dancing, of course. And also, number two, the outfits, number three, the solos, and number four, *My Life Flows On In Endless Song / How Can I Keep From Singing?* Can you put that on the agenda?

MELODY. Okay, there will be no discussion about the outfits, because the outfits will remain the same. They've been the same for twenty years.

MEGHAN. Twenty years is a really long time.

MICKEY. Yes. Mine has the balls of a moth.

MELODY. Okay, Lady Treble –

MEGHAN. Twenty years ago? Twenty years ago, people didn't even have, like, technology.

MELODY. Lady Treble, I'd like to hand a rose to each of you as a thank you. A thank you for having ideas and trying your best last year and this –

VALERIE. *(She's been prepping all summer and wants to get it over with.)* Okay, I have to say one thing about last year, I'm really sorry for freaking out and locking myself in the janitor's closet so that I wouldn't have to go on stage with you guys at Nationals.

*(****ALL**** are deeply concerned for **VALERIE**'s roughness to herself.)*

And you guys have been so awesome about not bringing it up that much anymore. Thank you *(She indicates that she's re-gifting her rose to the group as a thank you).* I promise I'll be there this year.

MELODY. This wasn't on the agenda, but that was really brave of you to talk about your unfortunate mental breakdown, snaps for you, Lady Treble.

(The girls all say "snaps" and snap their fingers in approval; this is a time honored tradition in the group.)

ALL. Snaps.

VALERIE. Thanks. *(gently)* Don't look at me.

(They turn away instantly. She's grateful.)

Thanks.

MICKEY. I have a thank you too, for Valerie coming back this year, we sound so nice when you are not singing in closet. Snaps. *(During these lines, she has handed to* **VALERIE** *the roses that* **MELODY** *and* **VALERIE** *had given to her.)*

ALL. *(all snap and say variations on this)* Snaps.

MELODY. Snaps to you Lady Treble, and remember you still have to get your permission slip signed –

MICKEY. Oh yeah, it's signing really soon. And Val is right; we could be beating off the boys if we sang songs with more, how do you say "has big balls" but for women?

(Beat, as they all look at her.)

KERRI. Lipsy.

MICKEY. Because we could beat them off with big fat lippy songs. You know, Metallica, *Welcome to My Jungle, Pour Your Sugar On Me*?

VALERIE. Wow.

MEGHAN. Oh my God, you guys, we're doing it. This is a sign. Mickey's right.

MICKEY. Really?

MELODY. Focus, Ladies we're not doing Death Shepherd–

KERRI. Leopard. She means Leopard.

MEGHAN. Okay, I would like to hand a rose to all of us and to Jesus –

MELODY. Meghan, you know that we all have different beliefs and if you want to make a point in a meeting you should –

KERRI. Eat it.

MELODY. – keep your comments non-dominational –

MEGHAN. – Fine. I'd like to give a rose to God, for helping us last year when Valerie freaked. And I feel like God always has a plan, I mean look at nature. And his plan for last year must have been that we would fail so big that we'd have to stop and realize that like maybe the reason we don't win at Nationals is because our outfits are so boring that the judges are falling asleep when we walk on –

MELODY. Look, Ladies, in any other year it might be legible to discuss some of this, but I think that because of what happened with our previous member,

(They all remember.)

we need to take extra steps of caution about how we portray ourselves, so that people don't think of us in a loose manner.

MEGHAN. What are you even talking about? Obviously we don't act loose or look loose and we aren't loosey.

MICKEY. Who's Lucy?

MELODY. I'm not calling you loosey.

KERRI. She's not calling you loosey.

MICKEY. I don't know who Lucy is.

VALERIE. I don't think Meghan's a whore. *(Pause.)* Don't look at me. Thanks.

MICKEY. Oh, Meghan is the Lucy. *(She nods.)*

MEGHAN. Oh my God, I don't even think you should propagate that kind of –

MELODY. The word is profligate. Look, Ladies, I'm not running a dictationship; we should listen to all the wrong points of view before we chose the right one. I just think that our sound and our image are part of the same ball of parcel: what the judges are looking for. I'm not saying everyone has to be really pretty, you don't. I'm not unrealistic. Snaps for sharing, Lady Treble.

ALL. *(without joy)* Snaps.

MELODY. *(Looking at her cards, back to the speech. She's practiced this before.)* Lady Treble, I'd like to hand a rose to each of you as a thank you. A thank you for having ideas and trying your best. But best is, of course, relative. We've been to Nationals the last two years, and we've never come away with the prize and the Acafellas have won each time. Why do the boys win?

(overlap, as all clamor to provide the right answer)

MICKEY. – Oh because they do fun songs.

MEGHAN. – Because they don't look like old fashioned mummies.

VALERIE. – No, because society looks at a bunch of boys singing and automatically thinks, that's so cute and endearing, but people see a group of girls singing the same song and wonder where are their boyfriends? What do they have against instruments? What's their agenda?

(All look at her.)

Don't look at me. Thanks.

MELODY. *(She was only momentarily puzzled by these unasked for interjections.)* – Because they have confidence. They have confidence that the group sounds good, so they do sound good. It's a self refilling prophecy. After yesterday's rehearsal it's clear we still don't have that confidence. So, this year, I'm not just giving you a rose, I'm giving you my confidence. Mickey, I give you my confidence that you can learn to sing a song using only the words from that song. Valerie, you will learn to be looked at while you're singing; I'll give you that confidence. And this CD reminding you that I'm looking at you; you can play it and practice being looked at. And finally, Meghan Beans, I know we haven't always seen with the same eye to eye but underneath that mess of unnecessary movements, you have a lot of natural undisciplined talent. And enthused asthma.

Yes, I'm the first three year pitch and president in our history, and yes I was Honorable Mention Best Female Soloist last year –

MICKEY. Oh yes, judge say you have very deep throat.

MELODY. – but we still came in seventeenth. A chain is only as strong as its weakest link – we saw that with Valerie's unfortunate panic attack. And we're seeing it this year with our background. So, I will sing backup. Meghan Beans, ever since our groups' insemination, twenty years ago, *My Life Flows On In Endless Song / How Can I Keep From Singing* has been our signature competition solo. It is usually given based on proven competence not just shrewd presidential hunches, but this year we're polishing every link. Meghan, I hand you my trust and our signature solo. Snaps to you Lady Treble.

(**MEGHAN** *is ecstatic and* **THE LADIES** *feel they're watching history.*)

MEGHAN. Oh my God, Melody, ahhh! I won't let you down. Holy wow, we are so coming together! Snaps!

(**MEGHAN** *hugs* **MELODY.**)

MELODY. Finally, in conclusive – if we're going to beat the boys, we need to work –

KERRI. Bitchcakes.

MELODY. – twice as hard. We'll extend rehearsals to seven, and we'll need to add Fridays as well.

MICKEY. Oh, no, I can't. I told him –

MELODY. Mickey, Lady Treble is a major extracurricular commitment. Tell your parents to pick you up at seven.

MICKEY. No I – it's not possible.

KERRI. And remind them about the slip.

VALERIE. Mickey, parents love a cappella; it's like a guarantee you won't get knocked up –

MEGHAN. I can give you a ride home.

VALERIE. – usually.

MICKEY. But –

MELODY. See, it's settled. Snaps, Ladies.

Scene Four

(Lights switch to **SIMON** *running through the aisle onto the stage to a microphone.)*

SIMON. They don't put up a list. They just go up to people on Tap Day and tell them yes, or no. I was in the bathroom when JB came in and he was like –

(Light Shift as **JB** *and the other* **ACAFELLAS** *enact* **SIMON**'s *induction into the group. They are singing the Billy Idol classic, "Mony Mony", which was a remake of the Tommy James & The Shondells classic, which was inspired in part by an insurance company, Mutual of New York.* **THE ACAFELLAS** *know little of this. But they do know they're singing it for* **SIMON**. *They do an elaborate Tap Day number that involved beckoning him into the center, "knighting" him, and then elevating him up into an Acafella. At the start,* **SIMON** *is not remotely sure what is happening.)*

[MUSIC NO. 5: "MONY MONY"]

SIMON. *(He interupts the singing.)* I'm sorry to interrupt.

But does this mean I'm not in?

Oh my God. Wait. Did I –

Did I get in?

(He joins the group and sings with them; he is finally an Acafella!)

Scene Five

(Lights change to the girls and boys all in the Music Room. All these lines are rapid fire.)

MELODY. Acafellas and Lady Treble!

KERRI. Excuse me. *(to JB who is in her way as she is moving a chair for MELODY to stand on to make her announcement)*

JB. *(to VALERIE)* Hey Sis.

VALERIE. Bro.

JB. You changed names again?

VALERIE. Don't look at me. *(She means this figuratively, for once.)*

KERRI. *(still trying to get JB to move)* Excuse me. It's for Melody.

MEGHAN. Oops, sorry, Jasper, I didn't see you there. You're so … quiet.

MELODY. *(unhappy with where JASPER and MEGHAN are standing)* Ladies! Fellas! I have a major announcement!

KERRI. *(to JB)* Move!

(JB moves.)

SIMON. *(to VALERIE)* Hi, I'm Simon Depardieu.

VALERIE. Don't look at me.

SIMON. Okay.

(MELODY has mounted the chair that KERRI provided.)

MELODY. Dr. Mergh consummated with me this morning, and now I want to consummate with all of you –

VALERIE. *(to SIMON)* Thank you.

SIMON. Okay.

MELODY. – as you know, Nationals has been getting bigger every year, and with all sorts of media tension, and well, after last year's concert at the Radio City Music Hall Annex, I'm sure no one could imagine it, but this year Nationals will be held – here, in Fellowes Auditorium because the boys are of course the defending National champions – and –

MICKEY.   JB.

No hotel?   We don't miss school?

PHILIP. Why did Dr. Mergh tell you first?

MELODY. and, and – well, this year, Nationals won't just be a competition, they're going to show it on MTV3; they'll televise it live! We will be watched by over a million people!

PHILIP & LASSITER.   MEGHAN.

Yes! *(They high five.)*   Ahh!!!! *(hugs JASPER)* Wow!

VALERIE. No.

(PHILIP and LASSITER realize they are looking at each other and turn out. JASPER disengages from MEGHAN and kisses MELODY's shoulder.)

MICKEY. MTV will love songs with woman balls!

JB. Dude, we're gonna be on TV, and shit.

(He fist bumps SIMON.)

LASSITER. Why would MTV show music? They only do reality –

MELODY. Dr. Mergh says there's an unprecedented amount of attention on high school singing now, and we provide exactly the sort of high stakes trauma that networks want.

JB. I'm totally gonna take my shirt off.

SIMON. Me too!

MELODY. Get undressed all you want, because we're winning.

ALL THE GIRLS BUT VALERIE. Snaps.

PHILIP. Ha! *(All look at him.)* What? Oh come on. They're never going to win.

LASSITER. JB, tell Philip *(gives gesture for, "Why are you acting like such a jerk?")* –

PHILIP. No, why are we always so scared to just admit we're better. We're the National Champions! And even if you were as good for girls as we are for boys, which you're not of course, you'd still be a girls group and they sound tinny. Everyone hears it.

(The girls react.)

SIMON. *(apologetically)* It's not tinny. It's just that we have falsetto, so we can hit all the high notes you can hit, and all the low ones you can't. It's a biologically fuller sound.

MEGHAN. We could be biologically better at dancing.

MICKEY. And having balls.

MELODY. And not being –

KERRI. Douchebags.

MELODY. – so conceited all the time.

ALL THE LADIES BUT VALERIE. Snaps.

MELODY. Come on Ladies.

Scene Six

(Lights shift to **LASSITER** *addressing audience.)*

LASSITER. MTV3 is a setback. I mean all anyone's talked about since is what color cummerbunds we should wear when we hoist the trophy on TV.

Last night, my parents took me to see the Philharmonic do Beethoven's 9th – with his original metronome markings – and for the first time, everything became clear. At first, we're sitting there, and I was just like, fine, violins; this is pretty enough. But then in the fourth movement I heard it. This whaa! The bassoon! It's the worst instrument ever, like this angry dying duck and I wanted to go up and wring its neck, to end the pain. I tried to plug my ears, but it kept coming through, whaaa, whaa. And that's when I heard them. The words. I mean, I'd heard the words, all along, but I don't speak German. I heard the words beneath the music. The truth. It's like without the bassoon, you only hear the pretty. But with the ugliness of that angry duck, you transcend pretty, into beauty, into art, into truth. That's what the bassoon was, a translator for the hidden truth. That's the power of music; you can hear everything – love and hate, war and peace, hunger and not hunger. Everything.

And that's the gift I have to share with the guys, and we have to give our audience, our parents, our teachers, MTV3 and the whole world a big fat wad of honest musical truth.

Scene Seven

(Lights shift. **MICKEY** *and* **MEGHAN** *walk the girls through the new rocking song they're proposing, The Romantics' "What I Like About You".* **MEGHAN** *demonstrates the dance moves, she and* **MICKEY** *speak-sing the lyrics together (though* **MICKEY** *gets them wrong. The projection reads, "***One week later***".)*

[MUSIC NO. 6: "WHAT I LIKE ABOUT YOU"]

MEGHAN.	MICKEY.
(demonstrating)	*(Meanwhile, what* **MICKEY** *says during this is:)*
OKAY, SO IT'S 5, 6, 7,	*(***MICKEY*** claps too.)* CLAP-CLAP-CLAP-CLAP
WALK, WALK, AND HIT THE FLOOR	
"THAT'S WHAT I LIKE ABOUT YOU"	THAT'S WHY I LIKE TO AH-CHOOO
FACE TOWARD HEAVEN AND UNDULATE.	
POSE "HOLD" POSE "ME". POSE, "TIGHT"	YOU SAY GESUNDHEIT
POINT TO THE AUDIENCE "THE ONLY ONE"	SNEEZING IS A LOT OF FUN OVER"
NOD YOUR HEAD "COME	IT'S TOO HARD TO HOLD IT TIGHT
WINK "YEAH"	YEAH
LET THEM STARE AND WINK AGAIN	
STRONG WIDE LEGS "IN MY EAR"	YOU SAY DO YOU WANT A BEER?
AND HEAD SHAKE AND HEAD SHAKE,	NO, I'M DRIVING AND NEED TO STEER
"CAUSE IT'S TRUE" PALMS OF JOY	OR EVEN – OOOH!
AND FACE TOWARD HEAVEN AGAIN	

AND "WHAT I LIKE ABOUT YOU"	HE ALMOST RAN OVER YOU
AND YOU RIGHT IT, AND YOU LEFT IT	HE ALMOST RAN OVER YOU!
"YOU REALLY KNOW HOW TO DANCE."	SCARED ME OUT OF MY PANTS
AND TUCK "UP", TUCK "DOWN", TUCK "AROUND"	HE SWERVED LEFT, RIGHT, ALL AROUND
RECEIVE HIS BLESSING	WE SHOULD
AND "TRUE ROMANCE, YEAH'	CALL HIS PARENTS, YEAH
AND WHISPER IN THEIR EAR	YOU SAY DO YOU WANT A BEER?
HIT THE FLOOR, AND 'WANNA" STARE	NO I'M DRIVING AND WANNA STEER
"CAUSE IT'S" PUNCH "TRUE" PUNCH	AND ACHOOO
"THAT'S WHAT I" TUCK 'N PUNCH,	AND YOU SAID GOD BLESS YOU
"THAT'S WHAT I' OPEN YOUR HEART TO THE SKY *(unbuttons her shirt)*	YEAH, YOU SAID GOD BLESS YOU
"THAT'S WHAT I LIKE " HOLD, 2, 3, 4. .	THAT'S WHAT I LIKE *(holds)*
"ABOUT YOU'	ABOUT YOU.

MICKEY & MEGHAN. Yeah.

MEGHAN. And that's the combination, ready to try it out?

*(****KERRI*** *is furiously writing down the choreography.)*

MICKEY. The song is so good, right?

VALERIE. Our parents might – Oh my God.

KERRI. Melody, it's 6:15. Time to take 5. *(She has the water bottles ready.)*

MICKEY. *(to self)* Jobete. *(to ****MELODY****)* I have to go.

MELODY. Mickey, sweetie, we're here till 7. Every day now, remember? We'll push on, thanks, Ladies.

MEGHAN. Wait, Val, do you not like this song? Kerri liked it. Mickey likes it.

KERRI. It's athletic.

VALERIE. It's not the song so much…

MELODY. Mickey.

MICKEY. I really have to be excused early.

MEGHAN. I know you guys are a little shy, but we said we were going to do new songs, and this is exactly the kind of new song we should be doing to beat the boys on MTV. We can't hide our lights under a bushel!

MELODY. Mickey, 7pm, remember? Meghan, wow, I could never dance like you do.

MEGHAN. Thanks, ready to try it?

MELODY. Only, I just realized what people were talking about.

MEGHAN. What people?

*(**MICKEY** has gone to her book bag and pulled out a cellphone.)*

MELODY. And, maybe if we changed a few steps, we wouldn't look like –

KERRI. Tulips.

MELODY. – what some people say some of us are, you know? *(without a pause as she sees **MICKEY** out of corner of eye)* Rules, Mickey, rules.

MEGHAN. Oh my God, I don't even know what you're insinuate –

MELODY. *(back to **MEGHAN** without losing a beat)* I'm not incinerating anybody. I know it's not fair, but people are –

*(NOTE: The portion in brackets is the English translation of **MICKEY**'s Herzegovinian dialogue that precedes it. The audience only hears the Herzegovinian, and should not be shown the translation.)*

MICKEY. *(overlap)* Jobete! Pet propuštenih poziva, arr Michaela. [Five missed calls, arr, Michaela…]

MELODY. It's really nothing, I'll show you, just minor changes, really. So it could be more of a, say, walk, walk, "That what's I like,"

[MUSIC NO. 7: "WHAT I LIKE ABOUT YOU"]

(**MELODY** *changes the dance [making it much more chaste] and* **KERRI** *hums "What I Like About You" while* **MELODY** *demonstrates.*)

AND GENTLE HIPS,
"YOU REALLY KNOW HOW TO" CLAP AND CLAP AGAIN
NOW "UP" CLAP, "DOWN" CLAP,
AND THINK ABOUT, HAND OVER YOUR HEART "TRUE
    ROMANCE."
AND WHISPER AND LISTEN AND WHISPER AND LISTEN
(*salutes*) FOR THE TROOPS "TRUE"
MAKE IT HAPPY HANDS, "ABOUT YOU" AND "THAT' WHY
    WE." HAPPY HANDS AGAIN,
AND, WINK TO THE NICE PEOPLE – SUCH A GOOD IDEA,
    MEGHAN.

MICKEY. *(whispering on the side, overlapping)* Jako mi je žao, Gorane, ali Intel Science Talent Nagradni klub je kasnio jer je nastavnik imao mali srčani udar, ali ja dolazim odmah. *[So, so sorry, Goran, but Intel Science Talent Prize club ran late because our faculty advisor had a very minor heart attack but I'll be right there.]*

MELODY.
"ABOUT YOU. HEY!" OH, GOSH, SURPRISE, "AT NIGHT",
(*breaking from the song to address the girls:*) I know, I know it's real.
And just a tiny tweak here,
(*resume singing*) "THAT'S WHAT I LIKE." FINALE "ABOUT
    YOU". –

MICKEY. *(overlap, whispering)* Ne, Gorane, prekinula sam sa akapela, sečas se? I Intel Westinghouse Science potraga za talentima je važna vanškolska aktivnost. Biću tamo odmah. *[No, Goran, I quit a cappella remember? And the Intel Westinghouse Science Talent Search club is an important after school activity. I'll be right there.]*

MELODY. Okay, that's the combination, great job, ladies, ready to try it out again? Why are you sit – Mickey!

MICKEY. *(overlap, growing louder)* Zato što je proba kaver benda Seks Pistolsa manje bitna od Intel Westinghouse Science Tima Talenata, i manje je bitna nego sve stvari koji mi ne dozvoljavaš, kao put za Washington DC, ili Matura/Polumatura ili akapela. Seronja. *[Because Sex Pistols cover band practice is less important than Intel Westinghouse Science Talent team, and it's less important than any of the other things you don't let me do, like the Washington, DC trip or like Junior/Senior Prom or like a cappella. Jerkwad.]* *(hangs up)*

KERRI. Ask about the permission slip.

MICKEY. *(starting to leave)* My plumber, he call, we have big plumbing emergency, and –

MELODY. We have rehearsal till seven.

MICKEY. I know. Plumbing is so bad, I have to go and do the how you say, uh *(mimes how she might fix it)* –

MELODY. Oh God.

Scene Eight

(The boys rehearse in the Music Room. **LASSITER** *blows pitches and they sing.)*

JB. Again? Dude, I don't know what you want from us.

LASSITER. Just the truth. Stop trying to sound so pretty.

SIMON. Okay.

*(***LASSITER*** *gives pitches, they sing, he encourages them. They sing The Pretenders' "Back On The Chain Gang", which as fans of the 80s hit might perhaps be quick to point out, is not actually about real chain gangs. However, the shoveling and pick axe choreography the boys are learning seems to belie that point.)*

[MUSIC NO. 8: "BACK ON THE CHAIN GANG"]

LASSITER. *(spoken)* Vamp it.

(The boys vamp, these lines happen over the vamp.)

Okay, that was good but it's still too pretty. Make it more – imagine you're actually on a chain gang.

PHILIP. Why would we be on a chain gang?

LASSITER. You've been incarcerated. You're on a highway chain gang. And you're working –

JB. I don't think this song is actually about –

LASSITER. – You're tired. It's hot, it's dusty, you can barely breathe, but you sing anyway. Why? Tell us. Sing your truth! 2, 3, 4

(The boys vamp continues. **LASSITER** *cues* **PHILIP** *in to start the solo.)*

PHILIP.
I FOUND A PICTURE OF YOU

LASSITER. No, what you'd sing *(singing)*
IN-SI-I-HI-HIDE.

PHILIP.
I'M SINGING ABOUT A CHAIN GA – *(spoken)* someone else go first.

LASSITER. Simon sing us your truth.

SIMON. *(sings)*

 MY NAME IS SPELLED SIGH-MUN

 BUT ITS PRONOUNCED SI-MO-OH-OH-OH-OWN

 AND I'M SCARED THAT MY MOUTH WON'T WORK...

 (spoken) It's hurting right now.

LASSITER. JB, take the solo,

 (JB flubs an entrance.)

 Don't be scared! Just sing whatever comes out!

JB. *(He rips off his shirt and sings!)*

 KIDS CALL ME DUMB, 'CAUSE I'M A JOCK

 JOCK, JOCK, JOCK, JOCK

 EVEN THOUGH THEY KNOW I CAN SING-ING

 ING-ING-ING-ING

 ALL THOSE AP ENGLISH PHONIES MAKE THEIR JOKES AND

  SNICKER

 DURING CLA-HA-HA-HA-ASS

 THEY THINK I'M DUMB AND NOT DEEP,

 BUT I LIKE PHOTOGRAPHY AND I KISSED BILLY HAYEK AT

  FOOTBALL CAMP,

 IN 9TH GRADE

 (They've all stopped. Beat.)

PHILIP. JB, Lassiter works really hard to come up with these drills, so –

JB. It was one time. For like four seconds –

PHILIP. – for you to go joking around and making stuff up is not productive.

JB. – What?

PHILIP. Focus –

JB. I'm not ashamed. Gay people are awesome.

PHILIP. – And tell Lassiter that maybe the guys would do less joking and take the work more seriously if we could see how it was directly connected to how we'll sing in competition.

LASSITER. This is how we'll sing in competition.

PHILIP. Jasper, could you ask Lassiter if we can't talk privately? Just the three of us? JB and Simon can practice blending.

JB. *(to* **SIMON***)* First of all, you have to breathe more.

*(***JB** *helps* **SIMON** *practice blending background notes while* **PHILIP,** **LASSITER** *draw aside.* **JASPER** *does not. Lights on them.)*

PHILIP. Jasper can you tell Lassiter that he can't possibly mean that we're going to sing like this at Nationals. I mean right?

LASSITER. No, Jasper, tell Philip this is just the beginning. We have to –

(They realize that **JASPER** *is not standing with them.)*

PHILIP & LASSITER. Jasper?

(Beat, as they stare at each other.)

LASSITER. Uh look, I know this is –

PHILIP. Ahhh. *(***PHILIP** *turns away in panic.)*

LASSITER. – Sorry.

*(***LASSITER** *turns away also. They both face out, shoulder to shoulder, not looking at each other. Beat. Then they continue talking not looking at each other.)*

I know that some of the guys in the group find this stuff pretty different –

PHILIP. *(overlap)* I know that the group can sometimes be tough to lead. It's just this is weird.

LASSITER. Art's not about normal or weird, Music is about shouting to the world, "this is who we really are, inside, deep down." You know? We've always been too scared to do that.

PHILIP. What if when people hear what's inside the group deep down, they don't like it. They wish they hadn't heard it. And we lose?

LASSITER. We'll win! Art always sucks at first, then it gets better. I promise the group, when we finally nail this, we will destroy Nationals.

PHILIP. And I promise the group to try to sing what's inside us, deep inside.

(They shake on it, doing a quick but complicated fist bump hand shake they have done a thousand times before.)

*(JB's loud voice pulls focus as he talks to **SIMON**.)*

JB. Think of it like kissing a girl, you know? Or a dude, I guess. And you're both like going at it full speed ahead, you're also listening at the same time. Not just to her breathing, and the radio, and the car squeaking, but to your hearts beating. And they're fast and in totally different rhythms but they're still beating together. And it's the same when you're singing in the shoe, everyone's singing their part full on, but you're also listening and even though the pitches and rhythms are different, you're still singing the same song – together. You know?

*(**JASPER, PHILIP**, and **LASSITER** have all been listening intently by the end of this.)*

| **SIMON**. | **PHILIP**. |
| Yeah. | Exactly. That's – |

PHILIP. – that's how blending works, everyone listens and matches the different pitches and rhythms. Thank you for explaining that to Simon, JB. Anyway, guys Lassiter's confident that if we keep working on these drills, we'll sound even better when we actually get to singing how we'll sing in competition.

LASSITER. This is going great guys. But it's still just beautiful-beautiful. Now let's make it ugly beautiful.

*(**LASSITER** has grabbed, and now hands out, a bullwhip, trashcan lid, cantaloupe and maraca. Lights fade on the boys.)*

Scene Nine

(Lights rise on **MEGHAN** *and* **VALERIE**. *The projection reads,* **"A Quiet Leafy Corner of Campus"**.*)*

MEGHAN. I can't believe she's making us do happy hands on MTV.

VALERIE. At least she gave up on *My Life Flows On In Endless Song / How Can I Keep From Singing*.

MEGHAN. Even the old people at church don't like *My Life Flows On In Endless Song / How Can I Keep From Singing*. Why didn't you vote for the choreography I proposed?

VALERIE. We'd look like uncoordinated strippers. Well, you'd look coordinated.

MEGHAN. Valerie, why don't you want a solo? You'd sound so amazing.

VALERIE. I know. But everyone would be staring at me.

MEGHAN. I wish I was stared at.

VALERIE. You are.

MEGHAN. I could help you.

VALERIE. Really?

MEGHAN. Yeah. You'll feel great about being looked at.

VALERIE. Okay because sometimes like I try mascara, but it never looks like enough so I put more on and all of a sudden I have like eyelash dreadlocks and I have to wash it all –

MEGHAN. Whenever I get nervous, I picture Jesus watching and let him comfort me.

VALERIE. Oh.

MEGHAN. *(in a "God" voice)* Hiiiii Valerie.

VALERIE. I don't believe in God.

MEGHAN. He doesn't mind. *(in a "God" voice)* Hiiiiiii Valerie.

VALERIE. Hi Jesus.

MEGHAN. *(in a "God" voice)* Hi Christian Soldier, you can beat the boys at Nationals.

VALERIE. I don't think it's helping to picture something I don't believe in.

MEGHAN. Well, just pick a person then, someone kind, and caring, and... when Jasper looks at you, it's like he's got this well of understanding, and you just want to see how deep it understands. *(beat)* I only like him as a friend. I mean he and Melody are great together, they're totally gonna last, and stay together like one of those Hollywood couples that stays together forever like uh –

VALERIE. She's a bitch to him.

MEGHAN. I know, I wish she would be nice to him....

VALERIE. They've never done it.

MEGHAN. Val!

VALERIE. JB thinks they've barely even gotten to second.

MEGHAN. Which one is second? Wait no, it's not fair to guess what happens between a boy and girl when they're alone. Like maybe she's kind to him, and loves him and he talks.

VALERIE. You should go for him.

MEGHAN. He is Melody's boyfriend, that is just – no, we can't even talk about talking about that.

(Lights up on MICKEY, who has snuck across the stage to one of the microphone and is excited to chat with the audience.)

MICKEY. Hey. Hello. Hiiii. My name is Michaela Dhiardeaubovic but I like to be called Mickey D and I love you the singing in the Lady in Red Treble. They are like community. I can do the talk you know, talk to other people not just my stupid brother who only talk about the Sex Pistols and wanting to play war doctor with you.

I love you all the girls but they get a little so uptight you know crazy about the this or the that, sometimes they have like a fruit up their butt that needs to be juiced. Melody needs to be juiced with the fruitness.

They have to loosen up and let it all hang, hang, hang, down and let the juice flow out, the words are not so specific, you know, let it out.

Scene Ten

(Enter **GORAN DHIARDEAUBOVIC**. **MICKEY** *may have to hide to avoid him. The projection reads,* **"Goran Dhiardeaubovic, Legal Guardian"**.*)*

GORAN. *(He speaks with the same accent as* **MICKEY**.*)* I hate these people who do the stupid! La la la. Is stupid. America is land of the lots, you can have many many instrument easy – so why are they not using them? No guitar, no drum, only la la la! ... Back in Herzegovina, I had band, we play the rock and the roll, hard, like a Sex Pistols! Michaela, my sister did the singing in the band. She have little problem with words but she have good voice for the rock and the roll, like scary old man living inside little girl.

But this was before accident, when our parents get, how you say, eat up by tractor? And here in USA, she say she have so much homework and no time for band. But I have suspect, and I follow her to school, and I live in bushes and peep in like Tom through window and I see, she have no time for Sex Pistol band but she have lot and lot of time for sneaker around behind my back and singing with this Ladies who shoop this la la this – a cappella this worse than jazz! If our father alive he never let Michaela make this disgrace on family! Now I have responsible for her so I will stop her from do the stupid, If she want to make a music, then she should sing in the rock and the roll band like real family!

(Lights back to **VALERIE** *and* **MEGHAN** *alone. The projection reads,* **"A Quiet Leafy Corner of Campus"**.*)*

MEGHAN. What about you, do you like anyone? Are you really a lesbian? You would look so cute with black lipstick.

VALERIE. Oh my God, Meghan Beans, I am not a – whatever, I might as well be. I'm not what boys like.

MEGHAN. Maybe boys are intimidated by you; no seriously, all the Acafellas are totally jealous that you have perfect pitch and they don't.

VALERIE. Except Simon.

MEGHAN. Simon. *(pronouncing it "Sigh-mun")*

VALERIE. Simon. *(pronouncing it "Sigh-moan")* He has perfect pitch.

MEGHAN. But it's spelled – Oh my God –

VALERIE. What?

MEGHAN. You like him.

VALERIE. I don't even know him, other than he's a freshman, and weird, –

MEGHAN. You do!

VALERIE. – and takes more meds than I do, and he has perfect pitch –

MEGHAN. You totally like him! That's so cute. You guys can like get together and *(demonstrates what two fourteen year olds with perfect pitch might do if they got together)* Laaaa!

VALERIE. Shhhh.

MEGHAN.	**VALERIE.**	**MEGHAN.**	**VALERIE.**
Laaaaaa!	Sssshhhhhh!	Laaaaaaaa	Sssssshhhhhhh!

Scene Eleven

(Lights up on the microphones.)

LASSITER. The Christmas Concert was amazing. We had a serious breakthrough.

PHILIP. The Christmas Concert was a disaster. What happened next was unavoidable.

*(Lights up on the boys in the Music Room, immediately following the concert. They wear Santa hats. The projection reads, "***Merry Christmas***".)*

JB. That was humiliating.

LASSITER. God did you see them? We totally shook them.

JB. I think the flaming dreidel probably scared some people.

LASSITER. Jasper, that bellow was perfect; God, that's probably exactly what the Israelites were thinking when they invented that song!

SIMON. What was that angry man shouting?

PHILIP. That was my father.

SIMON. Oh. Wow, your sister is super hot.

*(***JASPER*** gives him the "Dude, that's not his sister" sign.)*

Oh, sorry Philip, I thought she –

LASSITER. Sure it wasn't perfect, but wow –

SIMON. *(to* **PHILIP***)* Well, your stepmother is super hot.

LASSITER. – And we finally stopped being applause monkeys. They were –

JB. They were laughing at us.

LASSITER. People laugh at what they don't understand.

PHILIP. It's okay JB, starting Monday, we're going back to the old arrangements. Obviously, this isn't working.

LASSITER. No, starting Monday we have to go further, we have to build on this right away. Art isn't easy. Good art is uncomfortable.

SIMON. The girls must have been super uncomfortable because they got a really long standing ovation.

JB. Dude, making the audience uncomfortable isn't gonna fly on MTV3.

LASSITER. Forget about MTV.

PHILIP. Forget about MTV?

LASSITER. Screw MTV!

PHILIP. What about Nationals?

LASSITER. And fuck Nationals!

(All gasp. Pause.)

This is so much bigger than Nationals. Tell Philip he'd know that if he did what he promised and actually listened, you know, even once, to what's underneath the music, he'd hear it, the truth.

PHILIP. Tell Lassiter I am listening, but the only thing I hear is the audience snickering as JB nervously counts the beats until it's time to rip off his shirt and smack the cantaloupe, which isn't in my copy of the sheet music for *Back On The Chain Gang*.

LASSITER. Tell Philip, – no, I'll tell him. Jasper, stay out of this. Philip –

*(He makes direct eye contact. **PHILIP** tried to avoid it. **JASPER** tries to mediate.)*

JB.	**SIMON**.	**PHILIP**.
Dude.	*(to **JB**)* Do something.	No. Stop.
	(puffs on inhaler)	

LASSITER. I know, you're scared, I was scared too but if you just listen to what's inside you –

PHILIP. *(whisper)* No, Lassiter, what are you doing?

LASSITER. – and forget your Dad for one minute and really listen, you'll hear truth, honesty.

PHILIP. Honesty! You want honesty? Okay, who likes the songs better the way we used to sing them. Before Lassiter humiliated us?

*(**JASPER** tries to convince him to settle down.)*

JB. Let's talk about this tomorrow.

PHILIP. Lassiter wants us to be honest. Who finds these songs embarrassing? Raise your hands. *(No one does.)* JB?

JB. Dude, don't be a dick.

PHILIP. Answer the question, Lassiter wants to hear the truth, do you like the old arrangements better?

JB. I was willing to try –

PHILIP. That's not the question. Raise your hand.

JB. Whatever. *(Raises his hand. Flips the bird at **PHILIP**.)*

PHILIP. Jasper?

> *(**JASPER** looks at **LASSITER** and then agrees and raises his hand.)*

Simon?

SIMON. *(shaking his head in the negative)* Not uh.

PHILIP. Honestly.

> *(**SIMON** breaks down and nods in the affirmative.)*

Raise your hand, freshman.

PHILIP. Four Acafellows to one. Listen to that, Lassiter.

SIMON. Lassiter, I do like the whip part, it's scary but fun.

LASSITER. Fine. If you guys can't open your ears, I can't make you. I can't go in there and take out the emotional cotton you have stuffing them up. I can't make you hear the truth if you won't. If you want to, you know, sit here, and just win Nationals, just win, and never really hear the truth, and just, you know, sing pretty pop songs with nice arrangements that sound pretty and have the girls screaming and, and, and win Nationals, then, then, then you guys can go ahead and do that. Simon, will you give Philip the pitchpipe? *(starts to hand to **SIMON** but, like Richard II, can't give up the crown just yet)* It's still warm. Tell him to wait until it's cold and dead before he puts it to his lips.

(**LASSITER** *relinquishes pitchpipe and exits.* **PHILIP** *grabs pitchpipe from* **SIMON**. *Lights change, and as the boys address the audience from the microphones.*)

JB. He was a good dude, it's just the songs…

SIMON. He said he wanted us to highlight the siren call of loneliness that accompanies the omnipresent isolation of our modern world.

PHILIP. It highlighted we weren't going to win.

(**JASPER** *approaches the microphone as well, but the lights cut him off before he can speak.*)

Scene Twelve

(Lights up on **MEGHAN** *and* **MELODY** *celebrating post concert. The projection reads,* **"Merry Christmas".***)*

MELODY. Great job out there tonight honey!

MEGHAN. Ahhh! I can't believe they were hooting like that! I've never heard that before, on stage.

MELODY. Of course you haven't, that was such a great job for you! It's the best we've sounded.

MEGHAN. Val's okay, right?

MELODY. She says it's something she ate, but I think she was caught off guard by all that cheering.

MEGHAN. I know, I can't wait to do it again. Ahhh!

MELODY. Don't worry, we'll practice it tons, there's a lot of room for improvement.

MEGHAN. Oh.

MELODY. Oh, just tweaks. You were great. We'll talk after the break.

MEGHAN. Okay.

MELODY. Come on, let's go celebrate! Kelly's dad's gonna treat us all at Rosebud's. One scoop only.

MEGHAN. Melody, will you tell me now? I can start working on it over the break.

MELODY. It's so minor. It's the choreography. You just need to try adding a little less Meghan, and a little more song, you know, sweetie?

MEGHAN. Oh yeah, no, I know.

MELODY. It's not a big deal. Not everyone can be really graceful dance –

MEGHAN. I'm a great dancer.

MELODY. Of course you could be, sweetie, I didn't mean you couldn't. You're probably the most limber Lady in the group. Look, even though we're not doing it anymore, try practicing with *My Life Flows On In Endless Song / How Can I Keep From Singing,* no one can tart that one up. Just, don't be hard on yourself. See you at Rosebud's.

(**MELODY** *exits.*)

MEGHAN. *(as* **MELODY** *exits)* Yeah. Thank you. Okay, less Meghan, more song.

(**MEGHAN** *slowly starts practicing the solo to "My Life Flows On In Endless Song / How Can I Keep From Singing".*)

(sings) MY LIFE FLOWS ON IN ENDLESS SONG ABOVE EARTH'S LAMENTATIONS

(**MEGHAN** *tries to stand like* **MELODY**.*)

Argh, Why is it so hard, I sing better when I move. I'm not tarting. I can really dance.

(She's struck with inspiration. She looks both ways, and conjures up an invisible microphone and begins crooning The Contour's hit, "Do You Love Me", which she has memorized faithfully thanks to endless viewings of the movie Dirty Dancing.*)*

[MUSIC NO. 9: "DO YOU LOVE ME"]

(**MEGHAN** *mimicks the spoken introduction.*)

(Unnoticed, **JASPER** *walks in, carrying an oversized Valentine. He immediately turns around to leave. Her song makes him stay.)*

(He joins in and echoes **MEGHAN**'s *lines.)*

(Startled, she immediately stops and hides the imaginary microphone behind her back.)

MEGHAN. Oh. Jasper, I didn't think anyone was –

(He tentatively sings the next line back to her.)

JASPER.
NOW THAT I CAN DANCE?

(Beat. They look at each other. She pulls out her imaginary microphone and throws him one too. He puts

down his oversized Valentine and catches the imaginary microphone in mid-air. They both sing. And improvise harmonies.)

(They are holding hands and dancing their bodies towards each other. Before they meet, MELODY enters.)

MELODY. Meghan, are you still sing – *(seeing them about to be en flagrante, and JASPER's oversized Valentine on the floor)* oh.

MEGHAN. Melody, oh,

(She grabs JASPER's hand tightly. He doesn't pull away. Emboldened, she speaks.)

There's something you should know.

MELODY. Oh –

(MELODY picks up the Valentine and walks straight towards the new couple and kisses JASPER on the mouth right in front of MEGHAN. JASPER is stunned. He lets go of MEGHAN's hand.)

Are you coming Jasper?

(He nods his head, dutifully.)

Sorry, what were you going to say, Meghan?

(MEGHAN has no reply anymore.)

Can't remember? Well, we'll just leave you to defecate on it, and maybe you'll produce an answer. By yourself.

(Grabs JASPER by hand and leads him off stage. JASPER casts a look back at MEGHAN.)

Scene Thirteen

(Enter **KIKI TUNE**. *Lights on* **KIKI TUNE** *as she storms through the audience towards the stage. The projection reads,* **"Kiki Tune, Personal Talent Manager".***)*

KIKI TUNE.

Listen up, education comes in all shapes and sizes, and I am an educator. If I sign one of these boys, I can educate them on the world. I've got three touring groups right now, one in Vegas, one in Dusseldorf, and one in Scranton. That's education.

The truth is sex sells. You think people like listening to a bunch of boys turn a sexy Prince song into a eunuch's tone poem? No. But they love watching those underage Adam's Apples bobbing up and down, seeing those young hard bodies spank that song like a bad girl that needs to be disciplined, daddy. But there is sex everywhere you look nowadays, that's why you gotta sell the good sex, not the "I'm not sure this was really worth taking off my spanx control top" sex.

You think I'm wrong? You know my track record in this business; I found Syncopating Spunk in Orlando and turned them into one of the hottest acts in the country. Not this country, but Moldova is a hotbed of a cappella superstars. Don't let anyone tell you different. Five number one singles. Kiki doesn't go platinum by being wrong. Have you seen my house? It's a great house; it's the only pink, stucco, two story ranch in Florida.

Here in the US of A, a cappella is a firm, pink, ready to burst, untapped market. But you can't just tap it anywhere. You gotta tap it – tap it in the right spot and everyone goes home happy.

Look, with MTV3 getting into the act now, I gotta find the right boy and tap him sooner in the year. And I'm sorry if that means he has to give up high school, and singing with his group, and going to prom and introducing some debutante's tonsils to Big Johnny and the Quarter Notes. But if you want fame, if you want platinum, if you want stucco, then you gotta make choices. You want education? That's education.

Scene Fourteen

(Lights up on **PHILIP** *at the microphone.)*

PHILIP. It's been over a month since he left, and it's great. In fact, we're probably even better off now, free from all that constraining talent and domineering brilliance. The Fellows have really stepped up; JB uh… Obviously, we had to make some compromises, minor compromises.

(Lights up on **THE ACAFELLAS**. **PHILIP** *blows pitch.)*

JB. *(giving the mantra like* **LASSITER** *and* **MELODY** *do)* Alright, dudes. Sing it from your nuts.

[MUSIC NO. 10: "EASY"]

*(***THE ACAFELLAS*** *sing the first two verses of The Commodores' megahit, "Easy", about a man breaking free from an abusive relationship; at least that's what it used to be about – before* **JB**.*)*

(Their arrangement is lush, harmonic, almost angelic. It's tasteful like their other arrangements – at least it is in the beginning.)

(Instead of singing the next verses, **JB** *begins to freestyle rap to the audience – perhaps focusing on a cute girl, or older lady. The remaining* **ACAFELLAS** *are surprised [well not entirely] but continue to sing their beautiful tasteful background chords, turning the number into* **JB***'s slow jam.)*

ACAFELLAS.	JB.
AH AH AH AH, OOOOOH	
AH AH AH AH, OOOOH	*(rapping)* HEY GIRL, YOUR
AH AH AH AH, EASY LIKE	SMILE IS A GLOWING
SUNDAY, OOOH	IN THE DARK, OH IT'S A
AH, AH AH AH	SHOWING
JUST CAN'T STAND THAT,	MAKES ME WANT TO BE A
OOH	KNOWIN
AH AH AH AH, OOOH	YOUR NUMBER FOR MY
	TELEPHONIN'

AH AH AH AH
DONE ALL THAT I, OOOH
AH AH AH AH
I BEG, STOLE, AND I,
    OOOH

EASY LIKE SUNDAY, AHHH
THAT'S WHY I'M EASY
EASY LIKE SUNDAY, AHHH
OOH, OOOH, AHHHH

ON A STUDY DATE WE COULD
    BE GOIN'
TO THE LIBRARY, SEE WHAT
    THEY BE LOANIN'
AND I COULD PAY OFF THE
    FINES THAT YOU'RE OWING,
THEN CRACK SOME BOOK AND
    START A BONIN'
UP ON HISTORY OF GRECO-
    ROMAN
AND PYTHAGORAS'S THEE-OH-
    REM
AND WHEN HOMEWORK IS
    OVER 'N
WE'LL GO OUT AND LICK ICE
    CREAM CONE'N
OR GELATI, OR CUSTARD
    FROZEN
GET SO STICKY WE'LL BOTH
    NEED A HOSIN'
INVITE YOU BACK TO MY HOME
    'N
LISTEN TO THE GRAMOPHONE
    'N
DANCE UP BELLY TO ABDOMEN
TURN THOSE LIGHTS ALL
    DOWN AND LOW 'N

(**PHILIP** *leaves background, goes into the audience to bring a distracted* **JB** *back onto stage.* **JB** *returns, corralled, but undaunted.*)

ACAFELLAS.

EASY LIKE SUNDAY, AHHH
THAT'S WHY I'M EASY
EASY LIKE SUNDAY, AHHH
OOH, OOOH, AHHHH

JB.

BUT FIRST THERE'S
    SOMETHING YOU
    SHOULD BE KNOW'N
OTHER GIRLS I HEISMAN
    AND ENDZONE 'EM

(They rest while **JB** *finishes.)*
EASY LIKE SUNDAY
    OOOOOOH

THEY'RE IN FLORIDA, I
    STAND IN WYOMING
I REFUSE, SAY NO AND NO
    AND NO'N 'EM
BUT WITH YOU GIRL?
I'M EASY LIKE SUNDAY
MO'NIN'

(They finish the number as rehearsed, in tableau. **PHILIP** *is horrified by how the number has gone.* **JB** *seems quite pleased.)*

Scene Fifteen

(Lights shift. JB *remains. Interior of* **KIKI TUNE***'s hotel room.)*

KIKI TUNE. *(clapping)* Sunday morning, Monday morning, everyone's gonna wanna eat you for breakfast, dribble some milk on you Frosted Flakes. You're cute. Relax. You look tense. You want a drink?

JB. Sure. I'd love –

KIKI TUNE. – I'm just kidding. You're too young. And you're in training. Sit. Sit down. Relax. Get comfy. Rest now while you can, BJ.

JB. It's JB.

KIKI TUNE. We can change that. Can't we? Just as soon as you sign.

JB. But if I go pro now, I'd have to leave in the middle of the school year.

KIKI TUNE. Fame's not gonna wait.

JB. But I can't bail on the guys. I'm not a quitter.

KIKI TUNE. You quit football didn't you?

JB. They cancelled the program because of insurance costs –

KIKI TUNE. – Stars don't make excuses. You wanna be a star, right BJ?

JB. JB.

KIKI TUNE. You wanna sing on stage dodging panties at curtain call right? You wanna have groupies dripping on the stage door, right?

JB. But I have that already sort of, singing in the 'Fellas.

KIKI TUNE. Really, you got a lot of hot girls at this school?

JB. Oh yeah, tons.

KIKI TUNE. How many?

JB. A lot.

KIKI TUNE. Sweetie. I don't mean cute or mommy bought me pretty highlights, I mean totally smoking throw me down on the cafeteria tray and spoon me like tapioca hot. How many?

JB. Seven.

KIKI TUNE. Let's say two. Now imagine the two hottest girls from every high school in the country come together in one place.

JB. Like All Stars?

KIKI TUNE. Exactly. Like high school hot girl All Stars, and they're fighting it out for a drop of BJ. That's what the real world's like when you're an a cappella super-sensation. Sign.

JB. But I'd be ditching the guys.

KIKI TUNE. That's sweet.

JB. They're the ones that got me into singing in the first place.

KIKI TUNE. You don't wanna be a star, do you?

JB. Of course I do, I just wanna gradu –

KIKI TUNE. You don't have the sack.

JB. What!

KIKI TUNE. When you're with one of the two All Star hotties at this school, alone in a room away from the party, and you start checking out the grass on the field, do you say "wait a second, baby, I gotta go bring in the Fellas. I wouldn't want to ditch them"?

JB. No!

KIKI TUNE. Well when you're a big star, singing is what you do before you get the girl alone. It's like, "fore-foreplay"? You do it alone. Oh you like that don't you. Yeah, I knew you would – because you like your girls a little bit bolder. That's right, I've had my eye on you. I knew I'd sink my harpoon in your big whale of talent.

JB. Like Captain Ahab.

KIKI TUNE. Who?

JB. Captain Ahab, in Moby Dick.

KIKI TUNE. Lay off the skinflicks, kid, you're gonna need to save your hunk juice for performing.

JB. It's a book.

KIKI TUNE. Whatever. Sign.

JB. It's not a porno, it's a book.

KIKI TUNE. You won't need either when you're a star. Sign it, BJ.

JB. Whatever. *(He signs.)*

Scene Sixteen

(Lights switch to **LASSITER** *who addresses audience. He's carrying a sheaf of composition paper. He looks like he hasn't slept in days.)*

LASSITER. I feel great about leaving the group. Escaping. Great. It's probably the best decision I've ever made. I'm almost eighteen, so I'm running out of time to start thinking about me, as an adult, you know? With a legacy. Who I want to be, and what I want to do. For too long, I let my composing, which I'd like to start doing, take a back seat to all that pop nonsense. It's hard when you're in it, you can't see through that fog of cheesy pop arrangements, and intoxicating applause, and tight friendship, and crowd pleasing key changes, and pretty solos. I pity them. Now that I'm free, I can finally make my own music that's just completely, totally, really, not like that at all, you know?

(He drags a chair, sits, pulls out staff paper and stares at it. And begins to hum as he writes. Split scene, **PHILIP** *approaches a microphone to address the audience, as the remaining* **ACAFELLAS,** **SIMON** *and* **JASPER,** *rehearse in Music Room.)*

PHILIP. *(to audience)* Losing JB so soon after Lassiter left was like receiving two quick blows in rapid succession followed by a third more forceful punch; it was only two departures, but it felt like three.

(He leaves the microphone and lights rise on the Music Room. He addresses his troops.)

PHILIP. Okay, Fellows. I know it's tough with only three of us and one of us is mute, but we can do this. As soon as I learn this Tenor One line – *(sings)* WATCH HOW *(sings a flat note)* YOU?

*(***SIMON** *hits the proper note.)*

I can do it. *(tries to hit note)* YOU? *(spoken)* Okay, ready and one and two and three and –

(They start to sing the Tommy James and Shondell's smash hit. "I Think We're Alone Now"; though let's face it, it's more likely they know the song as Tiffany's hit in the '80s [from "The Mall Tour", of course]. **JASPER** *and* **SIMON** *sing backup,* **PHILIP** *solos.)*

[MUSIC NO. 11: "I THINK WE'RE ALONE NOW (PRE-PRISE)"]

*(***PHILIP** *sings the first verse.)*

(He doesn't hit the high note, he keeps singing. They don't.)

SIMON. We could transpose it down a step –

PHILIP. The arrangement is perfect. I can hit it. One more time. And, one, two –

SIMON. Maybe we ask Lassiter to come back.

PHILIP. Lassiter left us.

*(***JASPER** *steps in to separate them.)*

Because *(to* **SIMON***)* you infected him with your crazy freakiness, *(to* **JASPER***)* and you weren't good enough at his weird art project.

SIMON. I'm not a freak.

*(***JASPER** *nods to* **SIMON***, they turn and leave.)*

PHILIP. Wait, sorry, wait! Look, I'm sorry – you guys are great. I'll be fine once, we get to competition – stress brings your voice up at least a half step. *(They've left.)* You guys go, I'm just going to stay and practice a bit more. *(sings)* WATCH HOW YOU PLA-AY. *(doing a vocal warm-up)* CAW!

*(***PHILIP** *remains in the Music Room practicing.)*

LASSITER. God, talk about the bassoon.

(He continues to write and hum. **PHILIP** *continues to practice and sing.)*

LASSITER. *(crumbles up paper, starts composing anew)* Now that I'm not in the group, I finally realize how annoying a cappella singing really is, to other people.

(LASSITER continues to sing and arrange despite hearing bits of PHILIP in the distance. Split scene, enter SIMON at a microphone.)

SIMON. *(spoken)* How did I feel when JB left? Sad. Happy. Jealous. Happy. Bitter. Proud. Disappointed. Happy. In surrogate joy. I had a lot of feelings. JB came up to me in the bathroom and hugged me and was like, "Dude, Kiki Tune wants to sign me to a contract and shit, can you believe that man?" What could I say? *(puffs inhaler)* I said "Dude, I'm happy for you, and shit." We never got to sing our duet.

(He starts to sing David Cassidy's "I Think I Love You." He is too young, as are PHILIP and LASSITER, to have ever seen The Partridge Family, though JB could undoubtedly identify with Cassidy's heart throb status and crowds of screaming fans.)

[MUSIC NO. 12: "I THINK I LOVE YOU"]

(SIMON sings.)

(His song penetrates PHILIP and LASSITER brains. Unconsciously, they hum in their spots.)

(SIMON, PHILIP, and LASSITER all sing "I Think I Love You" separately in their spots. When not singing lead, they sing the background.)

(Fade out on the three in separate pools of light.)

Scene Seventeen

*(***TOBY MCCLINTOCH*** *addressed audience at microphone. The projection reads,* **"Toby McClintoch, Vocal Therapist".***)*

TOBY. When he opened his mouth at our first appointment, I could hear the fear of failing, the rejection of his father, the feeling of abandonment by his friend. They call me the voice whisperer. We have outside voices we share with the world; I hear the inner voice, the pains inside us, the desires. I think of my students like an onion, and I have to peel back the layers.

PHILIP. Hello.

TOBY. God, your pain. It's so deep.

PHILIP. I heard you can help me.

TOBY. I hear you can help you.

PHILIP. I'm sorry, I don't understand.

TOBY. I'm sorry you don't understand.

PHILIP. What?

TOBY. God, your pain is a like a chasm of despair.

PHILIP. I was told that if I came to you, you could help me.

TOBY. You should have been told that if you came to me you could help you.

PHILIP. I need help, I can't sing high enough.

TOBY. You need help, you can't sing inside enough.

PHILIP. Why are you talking like this?

TOBY. Why are you talking like this, Philip? We all have our outside voices –

PHILIP. How did you know my name?

TOBY. You said it the moment you opened your mouth. Your every word drips with it. You came into my office and your outer voice said "Hello" but I heard your inner voice scream, "Excuse me, are you Toby McClintoch the world famous vocal therapist? My name is Philip Fellowes the Fifth, no Sixth, God, I don't even know who I am, my father and grandfather have fought ferociously forever forcing me to falteringly follow in their furious footsteps and now I'm locked into a mutually destructive yearning yet unyielding standoff with the former pitch of, and my best friend in, our a cappella group, the National Champions, the Acafellas."

PHILIP. Fellows.

TOBY. That's not what it said.

PHILIP. I don't need friends. I just need help with my voice.

TOBY. *(correcting him)* Voices, Philip, voices. We all have our perfect voice inside us, and the more complicated our problems, the greater our emotional and physical duress, the greater the layers we have to peel through to find it. If you want to work with me, you'll have to be willing to peel back the layers.

PHILIP. Will it help me sing First Tenor?

TOBY. It'll help you sing Fifth Philip.

PHILIP. Can Fifth Philip sing First Tenor?

TOBY. Can Fifth Philip fill First Tenor?

PHILIP. How long will it take?

TOBY. A few months of sessions twice a week.

PHILIP. I only have one week.

TOBY. You only have one voice.

PHILIP. I only have one week.

TOBY. Nothing works that fast.

PHILIP. I need something.

TOBY. You can't cure anything in a week. Only two things work instantly in this world: love and drugs.

*(**PHILIP** spins and sprints to the exit.)*

Scene Eighteen

(The projection reads, **"Backstage at Regionals".**
Lights up on **LADY TREBLE.** **MEGHAN** *has finally*
found **MELODY** *alone and approaches her to explain the*
"misunderstanding" about **JASPER.***)*

MEGHAN. Okay, so like thanks for talking with me privately, Melody. I know you have a lot on your plate so I really appreciate it, and I really appreciate all the things you've done for us this year, giving us confidence, letting us try new songs, and you have helped me so much with my solo – and I'm so excited to go out there and sing it, and it really is more song now and I just want to say thank you, you know for all your help, and everything, and also umm about Jasper, I just really want to say that he didn't do anything, I mean I was all la la Meghan Meghan and he just harmonized, and that was it. It was just me. You guys are so great together, and totally compatible, you're both so smart and pretty and careful at driving and – I'm just sorry. I'd never do anything to hurt the group.

MELODY. You don't have to worry, Meghan Beans, I'd never let my personal feelings interfere with doing what's best for the group.

MEGHAN. Oh. Melody, that's great.

KERRI. *(entering)* Melody, two minutes.

MELODY. Thank you two minutes.

MICKEY. *(entering with* **VALERIE***)* Oh, Valerie have such big idea.

VALERIE. Kerri should sing. You know every part to every song.

MELODY. Kelly can't sing; that's ridiculous.

KERRI. Oh no, I couldn't –

MELODY. Focus, Ladies.

VALERIE. Don't look at me.

MEGHAN. You haven't said that in weeks.

VALERIE. Really?

MELODY. Alright ladies, let's go, with pride.

Scene Nineteen

(The remaining **ACAFELLAS** *shuffle out ready to sing,
"I Think We're Alone Now". The Projection reads,*
"Regionals".)

PHILIP. This arrangement is normally sung by five voice
parts. Know that.

[MUSIC NO. 13: "I THINK WE'RE ALONE NOW"]

*(***PHILIP** *nails the notes he had problems with previously,
and* **SIMON** *and* **JASPER** *are incredulous and delighted,
when they're not busy singing their parts as well as the
other two voice parts that are missing.)*

*(The boys finish triumphant, they've nailed it. They strut
offstage. The girls walk out in their formation.* **MELODY**
steps up to introduce the song.)

MELODY. Our next song is part of a special new direction
for Lady Treble. The girls convinced me to try
something different, and I'm so glad I trusted them.
This song is about friendship, about sisterhood. I'm so
proud to say our soloist will be –

*(***MELODY** *smiles at* **MEGHAN** *who takes a step out to
sing the solo. But then* **MELODY** *steps in front of her.)*

– myself. It's such an honor. Ladies. With pride.

(The girls are stunned. **MELODY** *gives the pitches. They
sing "Goodbye To You", the 80s hit by Scandal about
finally freeing oneself from a bad relationship. A really
bad relationship.)*

[MUSIC NO. 14: "GOODBYE TO YOU"]

*(***MELODY** *takes the solo, but* **MEGHAN** *is in denial and
tries to sing along.)*

*(***MELODY** *makes it clear that there is no mistake; only
she will be singing the solo.)*

*(***MEGHAN** *and* **MELODY** *battle for the spotlight.)*

(They each stand center stage, unwilling to cede the spotlight or the solo to the other. They steal lines back and forth.)

(For the final chord, **MEGHAN** *blows nose into a tissue in deepest sorrow. And perfectly on pitch.)*

Scene Twenty

(Enter **DR. MERGH.***)*

DR. MERGH. It looks so innocent, doesn't it? There they are, the future of America. Singing! But we poison them with our pressure.

A few years ago, at Whitest Academy, a school not unlike this one, they began injecting Botox into the vocal chords of their tenors; it quiets the dysphonia, reduces chord spasms, and prevents you from growing nodules as you tense for the high money notes. By God, those boys sounded like angels; big, husky, soprano angels. They won Nationals with a medley of "My Bonnie Lies Over the Ocean" and Justin Timberlake's "Bringing Sexy Back". People still talk about it to this day. But the side effects; drooping Adam's Apples, slack jaw, loss of all facial expressions – their Graduation Week musical was a disaster. The testing began after that. For drugs, for steroids, even estrogen. Because a cappella is a group activity, the testing is done as a group. The urine samples from each member of the group are gathered, poured together, titrated and tested collectively. They pass or fail as a group.

(He holds up **THE ACAFELLAS***' collective urine sample.)*

It's our fault. We say Bravo! Or Brava, of course, just not as often, but what we should have said is, "Sing. But sing for fun". But we were under enormous financial pressures: a contract with MTV3, the public demanded the returning National Champions, an auditorium to sell out. We should never have let them sing, but you have to understand – there's simply no way we could have known what was going happen next.

Scene Twenty One

(Lights switch to the Music Room and Simon is trying to find a place for the trophy on a shelf already filled with them.)

PHILIP. Try the bottom shelf. Or move one of Lassiter's arranging trophies. Or that stupid girls one, it's broken anyway.

SIMON. Ow. It's kind of sharp.

(JASPER enters.)

PHILIP. Was there room in the auxiliary case?

(JASPER indicates that it could maybe fit.)

Good, give it to Jasper.

MELODY. Hand it over Acafelons.

PHILIP. We just started rehearsal. You can practice losing when we're finished.

SIMON. Congratulations on second. That's really great for you guys.

MELODY. It's first place now. This is from Dr. Mergh.

(KERRI hands over a note.)

SIMON. *(reading)* "Acafellas, I regret to inform" – *(skipping)* Oh God – *(skipping ahead)* "collective urine specimen has tested positive for banned substances. Please come to the office immediately." Oh no.

PHILIP. That's impossible.

MELODY. It happened.

SIMON. I've never been sent to the office before.

PHILIP. We've never tested positive ever.

MELODY. That just means you've never been caught before. I wonder how many of these other trophies you'll have to give up.

(MICKEY and MEGHAN enter.)

MICKEY. Early rehearsing is much – why is everyone looking like you are looking?

MELODY.	KERRI.
The boys cheated.	They failed the urine test.

PHILIP. Allegedly.

MICKEY. Why? How much pee did they have to make?

MELODY. It's not how much they had to pee, it's how well, and please tell me you brought your permission slip.

MICKEY. It's at home, but I will definitely bring it to the tomorrow.

MELODY. If you don't have that slip, you can't sing at Nationals.

MEGHAN. Hi Jasper it's nice and normal to see you.

PHILIP. This is clearly a big mistake. We're the Acafellows. Our urine was clean. Right Jasper? Simon?

SIMON. Right!

PHILIP. Simon.

SIMON. What?

PHILIP. Simon is there something you want to tell us?

SIMON. We don't need drugs?

PHILIP. Simon? It was you, wasn't it? You're the reason we tested positive, aren't you.

SIMON. No, I'm a good person, I'd never hurt the group.

PHILIP. Really? The facts say you did. Fact: we've never tested positive before. Fact: you've never been in the group before. Fact: you have weird mouth problems and God knows what you take for them.

SIMON. No, I didn't take my medicine at all! –

PHILIP. Admit it! You just robbed us of Regionals!

SIMON. I didn't do it!

PHILIP. Admit it!

SIMON. No, I'm not a criminal!

MELODY. Jasper hand me the trophy that no longer belongs to the boys.

PHILIP. Wait, Jasper don't.

MELODY. Jasper, I'm asking you to hand me the trophy.

PHILIP. Don't you dare.

MELODY. Don't you not dare.

JB. *(entering)* Dudes! ... Ladies.

ALL. JB!

SIMON. You're back!

JB. If anyone's gonna have drugs in their urine, it better be me.

PHILIP. Thank god you're back, you can convince drooly mouth to confess so we aren't disqualified.

JB. *(to* **JASPER***)* Let 'em have it, we don't do asterisks. *(tosses the trophy to* **MELODY** *or* **KERRI***)* Snaps to you. Simon, did you take drugs before –

SIMON. No, I didn't want to hurt the group.

JB. It's good enough for me –

PHILIP. No. He has to take the blame and admit it.

JB. – and it'll be good enough for you; false positives happen all the time.

PHILIP. We're kicking him out before he does it again –

JB. If Simon goes, I go. (**JASPER** *backs him up.*) If Simon sings, we sing.

PHILIP. Fine, he sings.

Scene Twenty Two

(Lights up on JB *at the microphone)*

JB. Kiki Tune wanted me to lip synch. To another dude singing! She said he'd be the voice and I'd be the body.

Look, I know why she picked me. I know I'm not actually the best singer, or best musician, or even the best... guy. But I'm not a phony. I always thought of myself kind of like Holden Caulfield, in *The Catcher in The Rye*. Which is a book. Like he sees through the pretentious kids' bullshit, and has this really smart little sister, and gets in trouble at school and is all alone out in the real world. Like me with Kiki. I'm just like Holden. But probably a sicker athlete, and a little hotter, and shit.

But, if Holden Caulfield had sung a cappella with a bunch of good dudes, who had spent three years teaching him that singing softly wasn't a bad thing, he would have realized that even though they were total dorks, they'd become some of his best friends. And if for some reason, as part of his bildungsroman, Holden had ditched his dorky best friends and the group had fallen apart and descended into the wrong kind of drug use, then Holden Caulfield would go back to that school and he'd talk straight to them and get his a cappella group back together, and shit.

(Lights change to the Music Room. THE ACAFELLAS *come from all directions.* JB *has* LASSITER *by the collar, firmly but lovingly.* JASPER *and* SIMON *manhandle* PHILIP*.)*

PHILIP. Oww, Jasper, careful.

JB. Nice job, dudes. Put Philip there. Lassiter, you sit there.

PHILIP. What is he doing here? Why is he here? I'm the pitch of the group now.

SIMON. And JB is the quarterback.

PHILIP. And I'm the pitch, *(overlap)* and Lassiter is never singing with –

SIMON. *(overlap)* Quarterback is cooler than pitch.

PHILIP. What?

(**JASPER** *nods. Quarterback is cooler than pitch.*)

Oh this is ridiculous. Whatever.

JB. No, not "whatever." My sister's therapist taught us this really cool way of solving problems without breaking shit. You guys are going to sit there and tell each other how you feel and shit. Use the words, "I feel".

PHILIP. No, we don't need him or his stupid arrangements. We won!

(**LASSITER** *gets up to leave,* **JB** *stops him.*)

JB. *(admonishing and stopping* **LASSITER***)* Dude!

PHILIP. Let him go and tell him, of course he's walking out on us. The same way he walks out anytime he doesn't like the truth. The baby.

JB. *(this time admonishing* **PHILIP***)* Dude.

PHILIP. Jasper, tell him he's got a lot of nerve walking back in here after he abandoned us.

JB. "I feel".

LASSITER. Oh, that's ridiculous, Jasper, when the truth is he's the one that tried to kick me out of the group in the first place.

JB. Say, "I feel", first.

PHILIP. Jasper, tell him we don't need him or his stupid bassoon!

JB. Dudes! "I feel". "I feel". "I feel"! No one says shit, until they use the words, "I feel".

(beat) And no more talking through Jasper. *(beat)*

PHILIP. "I feel" like Simon should tell Lassiter that he left the year we needed him most.

LASSITER. I feel like that's total bullshit and Simon should tell Philip that I tried to bring something to the group, I tried to bring a gift, the power of music and he just ignored it.

PHILIP. Simon, tell him I feel like he wasn't bringing a gift so much as hijacking the group for his own stupid art singing project.

LASSITER. Simon, tell him I feel like he didn't even try to be part of the project.

PHILIP. Simon, tell him I feel like I didn't want to be part of the project, I wanted to be part of the a cappella group I've always sung in.

LASSITER. Simon, tell him I feel like I wanted to be part of that group and I felt betrayed.

PHILIP. Simon, tell him I felt ignored.

LASSITER. Simon, tell him I felt unsupported.

PHILIP. Simon, tell him I felt like we weren't going to win.

LASSITER. Simon, tell him I feel like there are more important things than winning.

PHILIP. Simon, tell him I feel like winning is pretty important.

LASSITER. Simon, tell him I feel like it shouldn't be more important than friendship.

PHILIP. Simon, tell him I feel like neither should art.

LASSITER. Simon, tell him I feel like fine he has a point.

PHILIP. Simon, tell him I feel like and – really?

LASSITER. Simon, tell him I feel like yeah, maybe he has a point – friendship should be more important than art.

PHILIP. Simon, tell him I feel like maybe friendship should be more important than winning.

LASSITER. Simon, tell him I feel like maybe friendship should be more important than anything.

PHILIP. Simon, tell him I feel like maybe friendship should be more important than everything.

LASSITER. Simon, tell him I feel like I really miss the group.

PHILIP. Simon, tell him I feel like the group really misses him.

LASSITER. Simon, tell Philip I'd like to sing with the group, if the group will have me back.

PHILIP. Simon, will you tell Lassiter he can lead my group anytime.

LASSITER. No, no, Simon, will you tell Philip he can lead mine. I just love being in the group as part of the sound.

PHILIP. Simon, tell him this sound just loves him being inside it as a part of the group. And we sure as hell need a Tenor One.

(**LASSITER** *goes to hug* **PHILIP**, *who pauses, then hugs* **SIMON** *instead and then turns* **SIMON** *to* **LASSITER**. **LASSITER** *hugs* **SIMON**. *Then* **THE ACAFELLAS** *start to embrace as a group*)

JB. *(starting their "Ahhhhhhcafellas!" cheer)* Ahhhhhhhhhhh…

ALL. Ahhhhh…

LASSITER. Wait, guys, while I was away, I wrote a new arrangement we could do for MTV.

JB. Whoa.

LASSITER. It's okay, it's just a pop song. No hidden meanings. I promised Philip he'd win and we are gonna crush Nationals!

ALL. *(put their hands in for the* **ACAFELLAS** *cheer)* 'cafellas!

Scene Twenty Three

(Lights up on SIMON *and* VALERIE, *sitting on a bench in a quiet leafy corner of campus. The projection reads,* **"Another quiet leafy corner of campus".***)*

VALERIE. It hasn't gotten any easier. It's like there's this entire auditorium of people following me, and I can hear them counting every freckle together in unison, seventy one, seventy two – and now there's MTV!

SIMON. Three.

VALERIE. Ah! *(beat)* Don't look at me.

SIMON. You could ask the audience to close their eyes?

VALERIE. That's stupid. Half of them would peek.

SIMON. Maybe you could hide behind Meghan, when she's moving side to side.

VALERIE. Melody cut the choreography. She just wants us to stand there, doing happy hands.

SIMON. You could skip Nationals.

VALERIE. I love singing. And I promised the girls I would be there. Give me what you take when you get nervous.

SIMON. But I don't take anything.

VALERIE. I won't tell anyone, just give me a little –

SIMON. I don't take anything! Not since competition started. I can't take my FlemCort because steroids are banned. Unless you have asthma; you can take anything if you have asthma. I really want to look at you.

VALERIE. God, I just need something. I can't go out there like this. I wish I could just wear like a wall, and just stand behind it everywhere I went. *(Beat.)* You're looking at me.

SIMON. I know. *(Pause, as they look at each other.)*

VALERIE. Huh.

SIMON. I know.

VALERIE. Wow.

SIMON. You could try a burka.

VALERIE. Those are culturally loaded! Don't look at me. I do wish I could be totally covered though. There'd be so much less exposed.

SIMON. Maybe you could find something that's like a burka but not so culturally loaded. Like a wetsuit?

(*VALERIE runs off.*)

Where are you going?

Scene Twenty Four

(Lights shift to **MEGHAN** *praying alone.)*

MEGHAN. Are you there, God, it's me, Meghan. I know you probably have a lot on your plate doing important things like ending wars, and hunger and lonely hearts, but if you had a moment, it would be amazing to talk with you? Because I don't understand why all this stuff is happening to me; between the dancing, the solo, and Jasper not being allowed to look at me anymore, Melody's making me feel like a little girl Job! –

(Enter **JESUS** *[who is played by the actor who plays* **JB***, wearing briefs. He speaks in a booming Old Testament-y "God" voice].)*

JESUS. I understand your pain, Meghan

MEGHAN. Jesus?

(He snaps his fingers, and the projection reads, "**Jesus, Son of God**"*.)*

JESUS. And, remember even though you walk through the valley of darkness, the Lord has given you the sparkle to shine your path.

MEGHAN. What do you mean, Jesus? I've been trying to sparkle all year, but the numbers keep getting cut! Melody is ruining everything.

JESUS. Before you point out the speck in your neighbor, Melody's eye, you must first pluck the log from underneath your own lashes.

MEGHAN. Oh I know, I do have logs, Jesus. I am so full of sin, and I know you know it, and I know you know that sometimes I even wish I was a little more full of sin, like college girls, with boyfriends, and I'm sorry for wanting that, but Jesus – Melody does have a log. She stole my solo!

JESUS. Meghan, even if Melody is a B – I – T – C – H, you can still turn the other cheek-

MEGHAN. But, she cut my choreography, Jesus! She's going to make us do happy hands on MTV!

JESUS. Jesus!

MEGHAN. And she cut *Goodbye To You* and is going back to *My Life Flows On In Endless Song / How Can I Keep From Singing!*

JESUS. Are you serious?

MEGHAN. Yes!

JESUS. You have to stop her. No one in Heaven likes *My Life Flows On In Endless Song / How Can I Keep From Singing.*

MEGHAN. But how can I stop her, Jesus?

JESUS. Remember, the Holy Words of the Bible, "She had it coming, she only had herself to blame".

MEGHAN. Oh my God, that's my favorite passage, thank you Jesus, you're the best! *(turns to hug him)* Oh, wow, you have washboard abs, Jesus. Just like, JB.

JESUS. Thanks. Remember, we're all counting on you, Meghan Beans.

Scene Twenty Five

(Lights up on **GORAN** *and* **MICKEY**. *The text in brackets is the English translation of what they say in Herzegovinian, and is included for the actors to know what they are saying. The English translation should never be included for the audience – they should only hear the Herzegovinian.)*

MICKEY. Hajde. Reci im. Reci im kako sve uništavaš svaki put kad steknem prijatelje. *[Go on. Tell them. Tell them how you ruin it every time I make friends.]*

GORAN. Jebi Se *[Screw you.]* Of course I refuse to sign the permissive slip to sing on the National MTV. She is big fat liar who lie to family.

MICKEY. I tell tiny skinny lie because I have big fat brother who is jealous pathetic loser jerk.

GORAN. I am not jealous, I am not jealous. I am protect you.

MICKEY. Sereš. Reci im šta si uradio. *[Bullshit. Tell them what you did.]* You should be ashamed.

GORAN. I am lot and lot of not ashame! I go to this school, and I say my name is Goran Dhiardeaubovic and I give my NEVER permission. Michaela will never sing with these Ladies who Tremble, these ladies who shoop, these – I like this, Melody… good body, good body. If she don't talk, I like her.

MICKEY. Sereš. Ti voliš sve što se mrda i ima sise. *[Bullshit. You like any girl with a pulse and a pair of breasts.]*

GORAN. Možda si samo zavidna jer ona ima super sise, a ti si mala ružna krava. *[Maybe you're just jealous because she has nice breasts and you're an ugly little cow.]*

MICKEY. Mmmh. Jako smešno. Jako smešno *[That's funny. That's funny.]* – coming from the boy who was standing over my bed with the camcorder touching his tiny himself while I was doing the sleeping –

GORAN. One time.

MICKEY. One time a week!

GORAN. Is one time I do that. Is one time. I was not touching. Ja sada govorim kravo debela! Ja sada govorim, ja sada govorim! *[I am talking now you fat cow! I am talking now, I am talking now!]*

MICKEY. Reći ću im kako si cmizdrio ako im ne kažeš istinu. Ili možda da pomenem torbu koju si zavezao oko sebe kada sam naišla. Illi možda... *[I'll tell them about your crying too if you don't tell them the truth. Or maybe I mention the bag you had tied around yourself when I walked in on you. Or maybe...]* we used to have a pet goat –

GORAN. Ne, ne, ja sada govorim! *[No, no, I am talking now!]* Look, I don't sign this slip because I have responsible for –

MICKEY. – and one night Papa hear goat in barn, very loud –

GORAN. Ne, ne, ne – Okay, okay, I uh

(MICKEY *bleats like a goat.*)

Razbiću te. *[I'm going to kick your ass.]*

(MICKEY *bleats like a goat again.*)

Okay. I will sign this slip permissive – If... and only the if this Melody is uh, she have good body. What I want is for her to know me better. Like happy naked sweaty peoples. So, this deal.

MICKEY. You will only sign my slip permissive, if I get the Malady to go on date into the Goran?

GORAN. Da. That is deal.

MICKEY. That will never happen.

GORAN. Then I send you back to Herzegovina.

MICKEY. But Malady will never enter –

GORAN. That is deal! Ya!

Scene Twenty Six

(Lights Up on the ladies of **LADY TREBLE**. *The projection reads,* **"Backstage at Nationals"**.*)*

MELODY. Mickey! Why aren't you dressed?

MICKEY. So Melody, now that you and Jasper break up, do you dating some one, some peoples?

MELODY. Mickey this isn't really the time to talk about my dating.

MICKEY. Don't get so hysterectomy. You should relax, you know back rub, soft music, go on a special date night with hunky foreign man.

MELODY. Mickey, what are you talking about? Ladies shoe up, we need to run through the opening! Oh my God, where's Valerie?

(Beat. They look at each other.)

Not again. She promised. We've got to find her.

*(***KERRI*** bounds offstage to look.)*

You were supposed to watch her.

MICKEY. It's not my fault. Sometimes I am so used to not looking at her that I don't even recognize her.

MEGHAN. The Lord is your shepherd, Melody; if you trust in him, he'll bring back the lost lamb.

MELODY. That's creepy, Meghan. Find Valerie.

MICKEY. Oh, hey, Melody, you know how I don't get you my permission slip for like really long time.

MELODY. Not now, Mickey. God, we can't do the background chords with just two of you.

MICKEY. Because I am having a very small confession.

MEGHAN. Melody, God hates happy hands and he doesn't want us to sing *My Life Flows On In Endless Song / How Can I Keep From Singing* even if it is about the power of the Holy Spirit.

KERRI. *(re-entering)* It's about friendship under adversity.

(re-exits)

MELODY. We are not changing the choreography or the songs especially because we go on in two minutes which is why *(to* **MICKEY***)* I really don't care why your permission slip was late, it's okay. Find Valerie.

*(***KERRI*** reenters from one side of stage and crosses to the other. She hears* **MICKEY***'s revelation.)*

MICKEY. Oh that's good, Because the reason we come to America is my parents get eaten by tractor and my loser older brother is now my parents and he only sign when I promise him that you will go on special date night and, you know... you will take him to funky township?

MEGHAN.	MELODY.	KERRI.
Oh, Mickey that's awful.	You what?	I'll go.

*(***KERRI*** exits again, still searching for* **VALERIE***.)*

MELODY. You told him what?

MICKEY. Yeah, I say that your love is like bad medicine. Really bad medicine.

MELODY & MEGHAN. What?

MICKEY. Yeah, I tell him that your milkshake bring all the boys to the yard.

MELODY. Oh my God, I'm going to be sick.

MICKEY. I was just really wanting to sing.

*(***MICKEY*** removes her beret, hands it to* **MELODY***, and starts to exit.)*

KERRI. Kumquat.

(She's arrived back with **VALERIE***'s uniform. They all see.)*

MELODY. Not again. But, she promised.

STAGE MANAGER. *(from offstage or a loudspeaker)* Ladies in Treble to the stage please.

MELODY. Oh God.

MEGHAN. God will help us if you let him.

MELODY. Not now, Meghan. Mickey, you can't leave, keep
   the beret. And Kelly –

KERRI. It's Kerri, turdface.

MELODY. – strap on the skirt.

MICKEY. Really, you will go on date with my brother?

MELODY. Fine, how bad can he be? *(to* **KERRI***)* You can sing
   her part right? Just don't do your 'thing'.

MEGHAN. Melody, God's giving you one last chance –

MELODY. You know what, Meghan, unless he can sing
   second soprano, to heck with you and to heck with
   your God!

MEGHAN. That's three times you've denied him!

MELODY. *(to* **KERRI***)* Whatever you do, do NOT let this be a
   disaster. Let's go ladies. With pride.

   (They all exit stunned, except **MEGHAN***, who pulls out
   the jagged, broken, Lady Treble trophy. She holds it up to
   assess its potency, and then exits on a mission.)*

Scene Twenty Seven

(Onstage at Nationals. The projection reads, **"Nationals".***)*

ANNOUNCER. *(over the PA)* Ladies and Gentlemen, pitch your pipes, and tune your forks. The moment I know we've all been waiting for. About to grace our stage, eighteen time National Champions, the one, the only, The Ahhh Cahhhh Fellaaaaaaaas.

(THE ACAFELLAS *walk on singing the opening vamp to The Jackson Five song, "I Want You Back".)*

[MUSIC NO. 15: "I WANT YOU BACK"]

LASSITER. *(Spoken to audience as the boys vamp, and* **PHILIP** *steps out to sing his solo)* This song is *I Want You Back.* Our soloist will be Philip Fellowes the Fifth. My best friend.

(Like everyone else on the planet, they love this song. It shows; they sound fantastic.)

PHILIP. *(He sings, then:)* Uh.

(LASSITER *gives the signal to keep going.* **THE ACAFELLAS** *keep the background and counterpoint going.* **PHILIP** *tries again.)*

PHILIP. *(He tries to sing, then:)* I'm so sorry

(speaks to audience) I'm sorry, I can't sing this song I – *(noticing the guys are still singing)* Guys, focus.

(LASSITER *cuts them off.)*

PHILIP. Lassiter tried to get us to sing our truth. And I was too scared of what people would think when they heard it. And I hid it. But I'm ready for the truth to come out. The truth is that I, uh, the truth is that I – am – the reason that our urine tested positive at Regionals. I snuck injections from my stepmother's home Botox kit because I couldn't hit the high notes. And I tried to blame Simon. I betrayed him, I betrayed the group. *(to* *the group, then to* **LASSITER***)* I don't deserve to sing with you. I don't deserve your friendship. Without me, you can still win.

(He walks off stage, through the audience towards the back door.)

*(***JASPER** *and* **JB** *look to* **LASSITER** *who immediately blows a note for the next song, so that the group can fulfill* **PHILIP***'s last wish. But...)*

SIMON. Philllllllllllliiiiiiiiiiiiiiiiiiiiip!

(Sings out to **PHILIP***. Much slower tempo.)*

(He walks off stage through the audience aisle towards **PHILIP** *at back of theater.)*

SIMON.	PHILIP. *(spoken)*
C'MON BACK I'LL SHOW YOU BOY	
THAT I KNOW WRONG FROM RIGHT	No, Simon, what are you doing, you'll be disqualified.
EVERY STREET YOU WALK ON	

(He reaches **PHILIP***.)*

(Almost hypnotically, **PHILIP** *sings the harmony with* **SIMON***.)*

SIMON.	PHILIP & SIMON.
FOLLOWING THE ONE,	I DIDN'T EVEN WANT AROUND

*(***SIMON** *leads* **PHILIP** *back towards the stage.)*

*(***SIMON** *returns to stage. But* **PHILIP** *hesitates before stepping back on to the stage.)*

*(***THE ACAFELLAS** *sing to him.)*

PHILIP. *(spoken)* Guys,

*(***ACAFELLAS***. all sing.)*

PHILIP. *(spoken)* If I get on stage with you, you'll be disqualified.

ACAFELLAS. *(sung)*
> BUT NOW SINCE I SEE YOU IN HIS ARMS

PHILIP. *(spoken)* My urine is probably still tainted –

ACAFELLAS. *(sung)*
> I WANT YOU BACK

LASSITER. *(spoken)* Simon, tell Philip it's not about winning.

JASPER. *(spoken)* Just shut up and get on stage!

(Beat of stunned silence.)

SIMON.	**JB**.	**LASSITER**.
Jasper!	Dude.	He's not mute.

> *(**PHILIP** jumps on stage and starts the song back up again; this time, they take it back the rocking tempo they'd practiced. They tear the roof off.)*

> *(The bridge. **PHILIP** and **LASSITER** duet and walk towards each other.)*

> *(**PHILIP** and **LASSITER** are face to face. The rest of **THE ACAFELLAS** sing their hearts out to the audience.)*

> *(**JASPER**, **JB**, **SIMON** and **LASSITER** strike crisp final poses, turned out to the audience.)*

> *(Swept away, **PHILIP** kisses **LASSITER**. Who is very surprised.)*

> *(Blackout.)*

Scene Twenty Eight

(The same stage at Nationals.)

ANNOUNCER. *(voice over)* Up next, last year's seventeenth place runner's up, the Ladies in Trouble.

MELODY. Lady Treble.

ANNOUNCER. *(voice over)* …Treble.

(Enter Lady Treble in perfect formation – with **KERRI** *in* **VALERIE**'s *usual spot.* **MELODY** *introduces the song to the audience.)*

MELODY. This is a very special song for –

KERRI. Nnnnn.

MELODY. – All of us in Lady Treble, it's our traditional number about sisterhood, *(***MEGHAN** *glares menacingly)* and trust. It's very special to every one of us.

(She blows pitches and they sing, "My Life Flows On In Endless Song / How Can I Keep From Singing".)

[MUSIC NO. 16: "MY LIFE FLOWS ON IN ENDLESS SONG / HOW CAN I KEEP FROM SINGING"]

(Enter **VALERIE** *in a hazmat suit. The girls make eye contact and rejoice. She rejoins the shoe. The* **LADIES** *sing the next verse.)*

(Suddenly **MEGHAN** *pulls out the jagged trophy from behind her back and holds it as if it were a knife to be stabbed through* **MELODY**'s *God forsaking heart. The scene changes to slow motion.)*

MELODY.	**VALERIE.**	**MEGHAN.**
Ringinggggggggg	Noooooo!	Rooooarrrrhhhh!!!

*(***MEGHAN** *swings the trophy towards* **MELODY**. **VALERIE** *rushes towards* **MEGHAN**, *knocking over* **MICKEY** *as she does.* **VALERIE** *grabs* **MEGHAN**'s *arm just in time and they struggle in slow-motion, knocking over the still singing, still smiling* **MELODY**, *and then both collapsing to the ground.)*

(Slow-motion ends. **KERRI** *is the only one left standing. She continues to sing* **VALERIE***'s background part.)*

KERRI.

BUM, BUM, BUM, BUM...HOW CAN I, HOW CAN I KEEP FROM SINGING, SINGING...

(She stops, looks at the audience.)

(opens her mouth, hesitantly) WHAAAA–

(softly begins to sing, then gets stronger)

*(***KERRI*** *sounds amazing; she is a talented, powerful and passionate singer. Moved by the power of* **KERRI***'s song,* **VALERIE** *gets up and joins her. Then* **MICKEY, MEGHAN, MELODY** *rejoin, the girls sing backup to* **KERRI.***)*

*(***MELODY*** *cuts them off perfectly.)*

KERRI. *(spoken)* Fucknugget.

(Blackout.)

Scene Twenty Nine

(Enter **MELODY** *and* **GORAN**. *The projection reads,* **"The Date".** *)*

MELODY. Okay. Hi, I'm here and I just want to let you know I am only doing this because you let Mickey sing at Nationals. And I should warn you that I have some mace in my pocket. *(then with forced etiquette)* So, Mickey tells me you're from Herzegovina.

GORAN. Yes. Yes.

MELODY. I don't think I've ever been –

GORAN. *(interrupts her)* You are so beautiful. You have the perfect bosoms. Is perfect size, no too big, no too little. Fit nice in hand like puppy dogs.

MELODY. That's –

GORAN. Sshhhhh…no talking no talking Melody. *(He tries to places his hand on her breast. She slaps him. He takes his hand away and drops his sheet music.)*

MELODY. What is this? Sheet music?

(She takes it and starts reading. Since the slap, he has suddenly, completely, and irrevocably, fallen docilely in love with her.)

This is beautiful.

GORAN. Da.

MELODY. This is my voice part.

GORAN. Da. I write for you.

MELODY. You're a musician?

GORAN. With instrument.

MELODY. Mickey never told me that.

GORAN. I show you my synthesizer?

(They stare at each other. She puts his hand back on her breast. Blackout.)

Scene Thirty

(Lights up. **MEGHAN** *and* **MICKEY** *are standing by one microphone.* **KERRI** *and* **VALERIE** *are opposite.)*

MEGHAN. Melody and I – we had our differences, but strong woman are like that.

And, Jesus and I, things are sort of, well, I mean, we're still always going to be really, really good friends, it's just that I think we need some space, and –

JASPER. Hey Meghan *(He walks across stage to the unoccupied microphone.)*

MEGHAN. Hey! Jasper! *(out to audience)* Everyone's so happy that Jasper can talk now. He's still pretty quiet. And he mostly just sings.

*(*JASPER *faces* MEGHAN *and begins to slowly croon Marvin Gaye's hit, "Sexual Healing". But although the song is in fact called, "Sexual Healing", he never actually sings those words.)*

[MUSIC NO. 17: "SEXUAL HEALING"]

MEGHAN. I know some people thought we were like…but there was nothing ever that happened, ever, I couldn't ever. He's an amazing guy, but I… We barely even have any of the same classes; that's almost like a long distance relationship…

(She tries to continue to address the audience, but JASPER*'s lyrics are infiltrating her brain.)*

He's great, but, I can't wait for you to operate –

*(*MEGHAN *stares at him.* JASPER *takes an imaginary microphone from the real microphone stand, and just like* MEGHAN *taught him, breaks it in two and tosses it to her. An eternity passes as she [and everyone else on stage watches] it fly slowly towards her. She catches it. And sings back to him.)*

MEGHAN. *(singing)*
BA-BY,

(**JASPER** *joins in and they duet and walk towards each other.*)

(**MEGHAN** *quiets* **JASPER** *with an epically big kiss.* **MELODY** *walks out, sees them kissing, smiles and approaches the microphone.*)

MELODY. At one point in my life, losing Nationals would have been catechismic. I kept trying to get the girls to sing perfectly like me. But seeing Kerri up there, I realized that if one star in a constellation seems brighter, that just means that star is closer to you. And if you looked from a different angle, another star would be brighter. We all shine, we just shine differently. That's really opened me up to a lot of things. Like Goran. God, my body used to be such a stranger to me.

(*During these next few lines, the cast comes on stage, and forms a big giant group shoe.*)

PHILIP. Well, Nationals was as a complete and utter –

VALERIE. Disaster. But sort of a hot disaster.

PHILIP. We were disqualified of course.

VALERIE. The only thing good to come out, was Philip.

PHILIP. My dad went ballistic. But he got really excited when Dr. Mergh told him all this would make a great essay to get me off Yale's waiting list.

VALERIE. We won our first Nationals trophy: Best Novelty Act. Dr. Mergh said we should accept it quietly.

(*Enter* **LASSITER** *who stands next to* **PHILIP.**)

PHILIP. And Lassiter and I, well… we can finally talk.

LASSITER. 'Cause what's the point of being best friends if you don't talk?

JASPER. Dr. Mergh says that singing is too much pressure, and we should do something more fun. But this is what we do for fun.

LASSITER. Man, you are going to meet so many awesome singing gay guys at Yale next year.

SIMON. And since so much went on this year –

VALERIE. And to make sure we don't completely screw up the same way next year –

SIMON. Valerie and I wrote an arrangement, to commemorate the year and be –

MELODY. – a perfect testicle of how we feel as groups.

LASSITER. *(holding up the pitchpipe)* And I read a translation of the libretto for Beethoven's 9th. It's not about making the guys sound like the bassoon, or what's pretty or ugly. It's about joy. It's about the sound. It's about the joy of being in the sound.

(He steps back into the shoe.)

LASSITER. With joy.

*(**THE ACAFELLAS** and **LADIES** give **LASSITER** snaps. He blows the pitches, **JB** starts with the beatbox, they sing Pat Benatar's "We Belong", and each takes a solo line.)*

[MUSIC NO. 18: "WE BELONG"]

The End

APPENDIX

LANGUAGE CHANGES

Page 16 onward: For the school version, **JB** replaces all of his instances of, "and shit" with "and nuts".

The origin of this phrase is explained in the inserted lines on page 16 *(below)*.

Further, these lines are replaced as follows:

> **JB**. Acaditions are really just a chance to get to know the guys and nuts –
>
> **PHILIP**. Focus.
>
> **JB**. Make sure you'll fit in, and nuts.

Page 17: Replace **JB**'s line *(mid-page)* with "He's just quiet, and nuts."

Page 17: *These lines are added after* **JASPER** *nods at* **SIMON**.

> **SIMON**. Why does he always say that?

PHILIP.	**LASSITER**.
This school has strict set of permissible language.	He's testing limits.

> **JB**. Nuts are on the list.
>
> *(continues original script)* **PHILIP**. Uh, guys, focus, we've got a schedule.

Page 18: Replace **JB**'s "Dude" with "Holy Nuts".

Page 29: Replace **JB**'s line *(mid-page)* with "Dude, we're gonna be on TV, and nuts."

Page 47: **LASSITER** says "And nuts Nationals!" after **PHILIP** asks "What about Nationals?"

Page 48: After **PHILIP**'s line asking **JB** to raise his hand, **JB** says "Dude, don't do this."

Page 63: **SIMON**'s quote of **JB** replace the lines with "and nuts" as follows:

> "… JB came up to me in the bathroom and hugged me and was like, "Dude, Kiki Tune wants to sign me to a contract and nuts, can you believe that man?" What could I say? *(puffs inhaler)* I said "Dude, I'm happy for you, and nuts. We never got to sing our duet."

On page 73, the following changes are found in JB's opening monologue of Scene Twenty Two.

Page 73: Change JB's line "the pretentious kids' bullshit" to "the pretentious kids' bull".

Page 73: Change JB's line "But probably a sicker athlete …" to "But probably a sicker athlete. And a little hotter."

Page 73: Replace "and shit" with "and nuts."

Page 74: Change JB's line (toward top of page) to "Without breaking stuff" and "tell each other how you feel and nuts."

Page 74: Change JB's line (toward bottom of page) to "No one says nuts until they use the words, 'I feel'."

Page 74: Change LASSITER's line (at bottom of page) to "I feel like that's total bull and Simon should tell Philip that…"

Page 90: Replace KERRI's final line in Scene Twenty Eight with "Nuts-nugget."

KIKI TUNE MODIFIED SCENES

Scene Thirteen

(Enter **KIKI TUNE.** *Lights on* **KIKI TUNE** *as she storms through the audience towards the stage. The projection reads,* **"Kiki Tune, Personal Talent Manager** *".)*

KIKI TUNE. Listen up, education comes in all shapes and sizes, and I am an educator.

The truth is – it's not the music. You think people like listening to a bunch of boys turn a sexy Prince song into a eunuch's tone poem? No. But they love watching those underage Adam's Apples bobbing up and down. You just gotta find the hottest Adam with the biggest apple.

You think I'm wrong? You know my track record in this business; I found Syncopating Spunk in Orlando and turned them into one of the hottest acts in the country. Not this country, but Moldova is a hotbed of a cappella superstars. Don't let anyone tell you different. Five number one singles. Kiki doesn't go platinum by being wrong. Have you seen my house? It's a great house; it's the only pink, stucco, two story ranch in Florida.

Here in the US of A, a cappella is like a watermelon; it's a firm, pink, ready to burst, untapped market. But you can't just tap it anywhere. You gotta tap it in the right spot if you want everyone to go home sticky and happy.

Look, with MTV3 getting into the act now, I gotta find the right boy and tap him sooner in the year. And I'm sorry if that means he has to give up high school, and singing with his group, and prom, and debutantes getting sweaty when he claps on the downbeat. But if you want fame, if you want platinum, if you want stucco, then you gotta make choices. You want education? That's education.

. . .

KIKI TUNE MODIFIED SCENES

Scene Fifteen

(Lights shift. **JB** *remains. Interior of* **KIKI TUNE***'s hotel room.)*

KIKI TUNE. *(clapping)* Sunday morning, Monday morning, everyone's gonna wanna eat you for breakfast, dribble some milk on your Frosted Flakes. You're cute. Relax. You look tense. You want a drink?

JB. Sure. I'd love –

KIKI TUNE. – I'm just kidding. You're too young, that'd be inappropriate. And you're in training. Sit. Sit down. Relax. Get comfy. Rest now while you can, BJ.

JB. It's JB.

KIKI TUNE. We can change that. Just as soon as you sign.

JB. But if I go pro now, I'd have to leave in the middle of the school year.

KIKI TUNE. Fame's not gonna wait.

JB. But I can't bail on the guys. I'm not a quitter.

KIKI TUNE. You quit football didn't you?

JB. They cancelled the program because of insurance costs –

KIKI TUNE. – Stars don't make excuses. You wanna be a star, right BJ?

JB. JB.

KIKI TUNE. You wanna sing on stage while they scream for your solo? You wanna have groupies dripping on the stage door, right?

JB. But I have that already sort of, singing in the 'Fellas.

KIKI TUNE. Really, you got a lot of hot girls at this school?

JB. Oh yeah, tons.

KIKI TUNE. How many?

JB. A lot.

KIKI TUNE. Sweetie. I don't mean cute or mommy bought me pretty highlights, I mean totally smoking cuddle me in the cafeteria and spoon me like tapioca hot. How many?

JB. Seven.

KIKI TUNE. Let's say two. Now imagine the two hottest girls from every high school in the country come together in one place.

JB. Like All Stars?

KIKI TUNE. Exactly. Like high school hot girl All Stars, and they're fighting it out for a drop of BJ.

JB. JB.

KIKI TUNE. That's what the real world's like when you're an a cappella super-sensation. Sign.

JB. But I'd be ditching the guys.

KIKI TUNE. That's sweet.

JB. They're the ones that got me into singing in the first place.

KIKI TUNE. You don't wanna be a star, do you?

JB. Of course I do, I just wanna gradu –

KIKI TUNE. You don't have the nuts.

JB. What!

KIKI TUNE. When you're with one of the two All Star hotties at this school, hitting the all night diner, getting milkshakes, do you say, "Wait a second, baby, I gotta text the 'Fellas to join us. I wouldn't want to ditch them"?

JB. No!

KIKI TUNE. Well when you're a big star, singing is just like getting the milkshake. You do it alone. Yeah, I thought you'd understand. I've had my eye on you. I knew I'd sink my harpoon in your big whale of talent.

JB. Like Captain Ahab.

KIKI TUNE. Who?

JB. Captain Ahab, in Moby Dick.

KIKI TUNE. Lay off the dirty movies, kid, focus on performing.

JB. It's a book.

KIKI TUNE. Whatever. Sign.

JB. It's a book. We read it in class.

KIKI TUNE. When I make you a big star, you won't need books or class. Sign it, BJ.

JB. Whatever. *(He signs.)*

GORAN MODIFIED SCENES

Scene Twenty Five

(Lights up on **GORAN** *and* **MICKEY**. *The text in brackets is the English translation of what they say in Herzegovinian, and is included for the actors to know what they are saying. The English translation should never be included for the audience – they should only hear the Herzegovinian.)*

MICKEY. Hajde. Reci im. Reci im kako sve uništavaš svaki put kad steknem prijatelje. *[Go on. Tell them. Tell them how you ruin it every time I make friends.]*

GORAN. Jebi Se *[Screw you.]* Of course I refuse to sign the permissive slip to sing on the National MTV. She is big fat liar who lie to family.

MICKEY. I tell tiny skinny lie because I have big fat brother who is jealous pathetic loser jerk.

GORAN. I am not jealous, I am not jealous. I am protect you.

MICKEY. Ma nemoj. Reci im šta si uradio. *[Bull. Tell them what you did.]* You should be ashamed.

GORAN. I am lot and lot of not ashame! I *go to* this school, and I say my name is Goran Dhiardeaubovic and I give my NEVER permission. Michaela will never sing with these Ladies who Tremble, these ladies who shoop, these – I like this, Melody... very healthy. If she don't talk, I like her.

MICKEY. Ma nemoj. Ti voliš svaku devojku sa pulsom i većinom zuba. *[Bull. You like any girl with a pulse and most of her teeth.]*

GORAN. Možda si samo zavidna jer je ona jedna zdrava žena, a ti si mala ružna krava. *[Maybe you're just jealous because she is a healthy woman and you're an ugly little cow.]*

MICKEY. Mmmh. Jako smešno. Jako smešno *[That's funny. That's funny.]* – coming from the boy who was in basement with the camcorder singing Madonna wearing my uniform –

GORAN. One time.

MICKEY. One time a week!!

GORAN. Is one time I do that, Is one time. It was not Madonna. Ja sada govorim kravo debela! Ja sada govorim, ja sada govorim! *[I am talking now you fat cow! I am talking now I am talking now!]*

MICKEY. Reči ču im za dinju. I za ormar u staračkom domu. Ili možda... *[I'll tell them about the cantaloupe. And the nursing home closet. Or maybe ...]* we used to have a pet goat –

GORAN. Ne, ne, ja sada govorim! *[No, no, I am talking now!]* Look, I don't sign this slip because I have responsible for –

MICKEY. – and one night Papa hear goat in barn, very loud –

GORAN. Ne, ne, ne – Okay, okay, I uh *(***MICKEY** *bleats like a goat.)* Ubiću te. *[I'm going to kill you.]* (**MICKEY** *bleats like a goat again.)* Okay. I will sign this slip permissive – If... and only the if this Melody is uh, she have good healthiness. What I want is for her to know me better. Like happy sweaty peoples. So, this deal.

MICKEY. You will only sign my slip permissive, if I get the Malady to go on date *into* the Goran?

GORAN. Da. That is deal.

MICKEY. That will never happen.

GORAN. Then I send you back to Herzegovina.

MICKEY. But Malady will never enter –

GORAN. That is deal! Ya!

GORAN MODIFIED SCENES

Scene Twenty Nine

(Enter MELODY *and* GORAN. *The projection reads,* "The Date".)

MELODY. Okay. Hi, I'm here and I just want to let you know I am only doing this because you let Mickey sing at Nationals. And I should warn you that I have some mace in my pocket. *(then with forced etiquette)* So, Mickey tells me you're from Herzegovina.

GORAN. Yes. Yes.

MELODY. I don't think I've ever been –

GORAN. *(interrupts her)* You are so beautiful. You have the perfect bosoms. Is perfect size, no too big, no too little. Fit nice in hand like puppy dogs.

MELODY. That's –

GORAN. Sshhhhh…no talking no talking Melody.

(He tries to put a finger on her lips. She slaps him. He takes his hand away and drops his sheet music.)

MELODY. Don't shhh – what is this? Sheet music?

(She takes it and starts reading. Since the slap, he has suddenly, completely, and irrevocably, fallen docilely in love with her.)

This is beautiful.

GORAN. Da.

MELODY. This is my voice part.

GORAN. Da. I write for you.

MELODY. You're a musician?

GORAN. With instrument.

MELODY. Mickey never told me that.

GORAN. I show you my synthesizer?

(They stare at each other. Blackout.)

REPLACEMENT SONG FOR SEXUAL HEALING
Scene Thirty

(Lights up. **MEGHAN** *and* **MICKEY** *are standing by one microphone.* **KERRI** *and* **VALERIE** *are opposite.)*

MEGHAN. Melody and I – we had our differences, but strong woman are like that.

And, Jesus and I, things are sort of, well, I mean, we're still always going to be really, really good friends, it's just that I think we need some space, and –

JASPER. Hey Meghan *(He walks across stage to the unoccupied microphone.)*

MEGHAN. Hey! Jasper! *(out to audience)* Everyone's so happy that Jasper can talk now. He's still pretty quiet. And he mostly just sings.

(JASPER *faces* **MEGHAN** *and begins to slowly croon Mark James' hit "Hooked On A Feeling", made famous by Reservoir Dogs, Ally McBeal, and Guardians of the Galaxy.)*

[MUSIC NO. 17: "HOOKED ON A FEELING"]

MEGHAN. I know some people thought we were like…but there was nothing ever that happened, ever, I couldn't ever. He's an amazing guy, but I… We barely even have any of the same classes; that's almost like a long distance relationship…

(She tries to continue to address the audience, but **JASPER***'s lyrics are infiltrating her brain.)*

It's not awkward, everything's alright.

*(**MEGHAN** stares at him. **JASPER** takes an imaginary microphone from the real microphone stand, and just like **MEGHAN** taught him, breaks it in two and tosses it to her. An eternity passes as she [and everyone else on stage] watches it fly slowly towards her. She catches it. And sings back to him.)*

MEGHAN. *(singing)*

I – I – I

(**JASPER** *joins in and they duet and walk towards each other.*)

(**MEGHAN** *quiets* **JASPER** *with an epically big kiss.* **MELODY** *walks out, sees them kissing, smiles and approaches the microphone.*)

(Scene continues.)